Acknowledgements

Praise be to God who created me with a vivid imagination and an insatiable love for research. He also created Miss Margaret Moody, who taught the book of Leviticus at Winnipeg Bible Institute and instilled a love and awe of the Tabernacle in my soul.

Larry Hadwen, retired teacher and advocate of God's Chosen People, took on the huge task of editing this book during baseball's off season. Thank you, Larry, for keeping me on track, catching my U.S. spelling, for your great insight and words of praise.

My five children, their spouses, children and grandchildren light up my life. They quietly endure my quirky enthusiasm for life, even when I don a costume, put on a red or green wig and embarrass them before the world. I pray that each of you will allow the Lord to have more of you than He has had of me.

I am surrounded by a host of friends, writers, mall-walkers, church family and facebook friends. Thanks for listening to me enthuse over all my research and a host of other things. I appreciate your encouragement.

Word Alive Press and Caroline Schmidt do all the work and do it so well. From the cover art to the finished product, I can't thank you enough.

If anyone questions how a leper could be living in Jerusalem, I claim artistic freedom. Jesus met a leper 'within a town' in Luke 5:12. Some versions use the term city so I dug out my poetic license.

To those who read this book. I hope it will provide some insight into what must have been a confusing yet exciting time when Messiah came on the scene. Emmanuel—God is with us.

Carol Ferguson
March 2010

Behold, A Son

Chapter 1

REUBEN WALKED ALONG the narrow street, laughing. He hopped three steps on one foot and three steps on the other foot. Then he ran for a while, stopped, turned around and walked backwards. He skipped and chuckled out loud when he realized he still knew how. He was a bit embarrassed to be acting like this when he had passed sixteen years already but it had been a long time since he had done these things. He looked in amazement at his hands and feet. He counted ten fingers, bending each one as he counted. He counted ten toes, surprised to see that he even had toenails. He touched his ears and pinched his ear lobes until they hurt and then he laughed again. Everything was the way it used to be.

The only things that remained of his life as a leper beggar were the dirty ragged clothes he wore, his filthy matted hair and the grimy dirt on his arms and legs. He almost burst as the desire to tell someone swelled within him. *Perhaps I should go back to the inn and tell Tirus.* As he thought about doing that the small shops in the market place caught his attention. He had lived the isolated life of a leper for so long that curiosity pulled him to explore this bustling part of the city.

Thousands of people who had come to celebrate Passover were streaming in all directions through the streets of Jerusalem. Donkeys were burdened down with every imaginable load and women walked by balancing belongings on their heads. Not once since he came to Jerusalem had Reuben been free to wander through the markets, visit the temple or take part in the festivities.

He stopped at a stall heaped high with woolen blankets. Accustomed to sitting motionless and unnoticed, he now stood at the end of the stall for several moments, nothing moving except ten fingers gently caressing the soft blankets that hung over the edge of the table. Slowly he inched his way along to where he could touch the colourful embroidered silk garments displayed in another booth, such a different texture than the wool. Gently grasping a piece of silk, he rubbed the material back and forth between his fingers, closing his eyes to concentrate on the fold that slipped and slid in his dirty hand.

"Get away! Don't touch the silk!" A man came at Reuben with his arm raised to strike him but Reuben darted away and disappeared into the crowd.

"Tirus! Look!" Reuben yelled at a man coming towards him minutes later. "A man touched me! No one has touched me for more than four years. It was that man who has been healing people." Reuben paused to catch his breath. "He put his hand on me and my leprosy is gone! Look!"

"Who are you?" Tirus, a local innkeeper turned and stared at Reuben.

"I'm Reuben, the leper boy, who sits on your doorstep. But the leprosy is all gone. Look at my hands and my feet, my ears, my skin. Every part is healed."

Reuben stood unmoving as the man's eyes roamed over him from the matted hair on his head to the dirt-encrusted toes. Reuben knew exactly when Tirus recognized the filthy rags that hung on his slight frame because his eyes suddenly opened wide.

"Is it really you? You are so tall? Have you showed yourself to the priest? Only the priest can declare you clean."

"Where do I go? What do I say? Will they make me go and dunk myself in the river seven times like Naaman the leper did? That would be good because I need a bath." Reuben twitched in excitement. "Can you show me the way?" Reuben had spent more than four years here in Jerusalem curled up in front of this man's inn, calling out to warn people not to touch him, begging for what bits of food would be thrown his way.

Lepers were not normally allowed in the city but when Tirus had found eleven-year-old Reuben crouched on the steps of his inn his heart melted. He told him he could stay there if he didn't move and contaminate any other areas. He was one of the few people who took pity on Reuben, giving him scraps from his own table on days when no one else had offered him any.

"I will take you. Come!" Tirus pointed and began walking in the direction of the Temple Mount. Covering over 30 acres at the highest point of the city, it was the center of their lives. Today the Temple, which housed the Holy Place and the Holy of Holies, gleamed as the sunshine reflected off its creamy white walls.

"That prophet, Jesus, must be the Messiah, don't you think?" Reuben strode along beside the innkeeper, glancing at this man who meant so much to him. Tirus leaped to the side, avoiding contact as Reuben waved his arms in excitement.

"Don't let anyone hear you say that," Tirus stated in a loud whisper, "especially not the priest. That will get you in trouble." They walked quickly down a steep street in Jerusalem and headed up the other side. Reuben was surprised that he had no trouble keeping up with the man's long stride.

Reuben glanced from side to side, his heart thumping faster when they arrived at the Temple Mount. He hesitated before following Tirus up the huge staircase, through a double gate and into an enormous portico where he had never been before.

Tilting his head back, Reuben looked up, way up, amazed at the four rows of soaring white marble columns, so big he was sure it would take two men to reach their arms around one. He could hardly take his eyes off the intricate carvings in the beautiful wooden ceiling covering a seemingly endless walkway.

"Anyone can enter this area," Tirus stated, sensing that the boy had never been on the Temple Mount before. "But there is another area where only circumcised Israelites are allowed."

"Come!" Tirus interrupted Reuben's sight seeing. His steps echoed on the stone floor as they walked and walked and walked, Reuben's bare feet slapped on the stone. Hundreds of people scurried about, each one taking care of their own private errands, paying their temple tax, bringing a praise offering or being cleansed. Through a gap in the crowd Reuben saw a large open-air court but they bypassed it, and then turned left and walked along another walkway until they came to a smaller gate.

"Wait here. I will go into the Court of the Israelites and find a priest."

Reuben noticed people staring at his rags. Looking around he realized the area Tirus had entered was open to the sky above, unlike the porches that surrounded it on three sides. He could see the tallest of all the building, The Most Holy Place, covered over, protected from the sun and rain.

Tirus glanced back over his shoulder as he went through the gate. *He's probably making sure I don't go anywhere.* The innkeeper disappeared further into the temple area but his voice echoed and Reuben could hear him talking to someone.

"There is a leper outside the gate who wants to be declared clean."

"What? Another one?"

Reuben waited, rocking from one foot to the other in anticipation. The priest would take one look at him and declare him healed and he could go home, back to his own mama and papa, his brothers and his sister. He had not seen any of them for a long time.

Tirus reappeared with a priest following, shaking his head in frustration. Reuben had never been this close to a priest before. He stared at the man in awe.

"Who are you?" The priest asked. "What do you want?"

"I am Reuben, the leper who used to beg outside the inn. I've been healed."

"Hold out your arms. Lift your robe so I can see your legs." The priest glanced at Reuben, but never touched him. Then he started talking.

"Go and get what you need for cleansing: two doves, cedar wood, a scarlet cord and a twig of hyssop and make sure the birds are alive and clean. Bring them back here and after the sacrifices are made I will declare you clean. Then you will have to separate yourself for another seven days and return with a lamb for a trespass offering, two more birds for a sin offering and a burnt offering, as well as flour and oil. That's what The Law demands." Having said all that he took a breath, pulled his robes close around himself, turned and disappeared through the gate.

Reuben stared after him in confusion. He didn't understand half of what the man had rattled off but he knew he had not declared him cleansed.

"We'll be back soon," Tirus called after him and quickly turned and started retracing their steps. "Come!" Reuben followed close behind the innkeeper, asking questions.

"What did he say? Where can I catch two birds? I don't have a scarlet cord. Why do I need hyssop? Where can I get flour and oil and how much do I need? What did he say about a piece of cedar?" They walked the whole distance through the porch again to where they had first entered the Temple Mount.

He almost ran into Tirus when the man came to an abrupt stop. Reuben had been so busy looking around that he hadn't noticed the merchants who had a variety of articles for sale and the moneychangers who were busy redeeming Roman coins people could not use in the temple. *I don't have any money to buy all the things I need,* Reuben thought as he saw Tirus finger a small bag of money tied at his waist.

TIRUS BEGAN LOOKING AROUND for what they needed. *If my friend Ethan were here he wouldn't think twice about helping the lad. The only thing I will get out of this is a clean spot on the steps of my inn. At least I won't feel guilty looking at the boy with his dirty shaggy hair, grubby rags and stubby fingers and toes. And I won't smell him every time the wind blows in the wrong direction. I guess that is worth a few coins.*

✡ ✡ ✡

"LOOK! BIRDS." Reuben crouched down before a cage full of doves. "How do we know if they're clean?"

"These birds are clean under the law," the merchant shouted at him, "suitable for sacrifice. Get your dirty fingers off of them!" Reuben wasn't startled, he was used to people yelling and cursing at him.

Tirus paid for two birds and Reuben quickly snatched the little covered basket the man held out towards Tirus. He wanted to hold onto these birds that would buy him a clean life. They moved from stall to stall as Tirus bought a twig of cedar, a bunch of hyssop and a scarlet cord.

"Why do I need all these things?" Reuben asked on the long walk back to the gate where the priest had come out to see him.

"The cedar symbolizes strength and it never rots," he stated, showing Reuben the cedar twig. "It grows bigger than any other tree. Hyssop is the smallest tree, but its sweet minty scent symbolizes the taking away of the smell of decaying flesh." Tirus sniffed as he turned his face towards Reuben. Stale dirt and sweat hung on the air, but the gagging, breathtaking smell of decaying flesh was gone. "These two kinds of wood, the largest and the smallest remind us how The Law covers the greatest and the least of people."

Tirus dangled the red cord in front of Reuben's face. "The red cord reminds us of the lamb's blood painted on the doorposts with hyssop that saved our people in Egypt. "You will see what the priest does with all of it."

Chapter 2

REUBEN NOTED THE SURPRISE on the priest's face when they arrived back so soon but the man immediately fetched a bowl of spring water. Reuben grimaced as the priest held one of the birds over the water and slit its throat with a sharp knife. The water in the bowl turned pink. Then the priest grabbed the scarlet cord and used it to tie the second bird and the sprig of hyssop to the cedar twig like a bouquet and dipped them into the blood-tinged water. Water clung to the hairy leaves and branches of the hyssop as the priest lifted the bundle and waved it toward Reuben. Startled, the bird shook its water-drenched head and Reuben was startled as well when the first drops hit him. Seven times the priest sprayed him and by then the bloody water had dribbled down Reuben's face and was running down his neck. With a flick of his wrist the priest untied the cord and released the bird.

"You are now clean," the priest stated as the bird stretched its wings, leapt into air and flew away.

Reuben looked at his arms, where the water droplets had left clean trails and blotches in the dirt. He grinned. He was only kind of clean.

"That was easier than dipping in a river. I can go now, yes?" *Maybe I can find a river to take a bath in.*

"Wash your clothes, shave every hair off your body and then bathe yourself. I already told you that you have to remain separated from everyone for another seven days and come back with a lamb, two doves, flour and oil. The lamb will be for a trespass offering and the two birds for the sin and burnt offerings. Go!" His long, well-groomed finger pointed away from the temple.

"Where can I go to wash?" Reuben looked to Tirus for an answer but the man had already followed the priest farther into the temple. *I didn't even get to thank him.*

"I heard!" A man whispered as he came near to Reuben. "I too have been cleansed from leprosy. Come! I will help you."

Reuben followed the man because he didn't know what else to do. Back through the outer courts of the Temple Mount they walked, down onto the streets of Jerusalem and then Reuben had to walk fast to keep up to the man as they headed south through the narrow hilly streets of the city. They passed several towers and monuments until finally they exited the city through the west gate and made a left turn.

"Where are we going?" Reuben finally asked as they walked along the outside of the city wall.

"Here! This is called the Serpent's Pool and you can wash here. Then I will shave you."

"I don't have a razor."

"I have one. A friend gave it to me and it is my ministry for the Lord. He also gave me a bit of soap." He held out a small square of soap. Reuben took it and walked down into the pool, taking off his filthy clothes as he went.

Awkwardly he washed his clothes, threw them out on the ground to dry and then began to wash layers of filth off his own body. Down under the water he sank, relaxing, enjoying the soft feel of the water washing over him, another thing that had been denied him for more than four years.

"The Law says you have to submerge yourself three times," the man called to him. So three times Reuben disappeared under the water. He soaped his head, arms and legs, scrubbing the filth off every inch of flesh, surprised to realize how long his arms and legs were, reveling in the soap sliding over his body.

Finally, dressed in clean, but wet, clothing, Reuben was directed to sit on a rock. He shivered when he saw the sharp flat blade in the man's hand. *I'm glad I don't have to shave myself. I wouldn't even know which direction to move the blade.*

Talking as he worked, the man began to shave Reuben's head. One by one tangled black curls fell to the ground. This man was quite vocal about his own belief that only the Messiah could have healed them both. They discussed the prophet who was doing these miracles in the city and soon Reuben was sharing his story, glad to finally talk to someone who understood.

"Hold still!" A warm human hand on his head startled Reuben as his head was tilted from side to side. He was startled again when the man again clamped the huge hand on his shaved head and tipped it backwards.

"Don't move. I have to shave off your eyebrows."

Reuben froze in place as the razor came towards his eye. Two swipes on each side and his eyebrows were gone. Reuben felt the top of his head and his bald forehead where his eyebrows once grew. He was thankful he had no hair on his arms, legs or in his ears like some old men had.

"Now you have to be back at the temple in seven days with your offering," the man stated as he folded the razor.

"I want to go home," Reuben stated. "I don't want to sit in front of the inn. I want my mother. She will be so happy to see me." Reuben realized as he made those statements that he still sounded like the eleven-year-old boy who left home over four years ago rather than a sixteen-year-old young man.

"It would be good to tell your parents what has happened. They can supply a lamb for you, flour and oil and two more birds. I'll buy you a cheese blintz to eat along the way. But first I will pray for you."

Once again the man placed his hand on top of Reuben's head and began to pray. It was like no prayer Reuben had ever heard. The man praised and gave honour to the creator for what he had made. He prayed for sustenance, for forgiveness, for safety for Reuben as he traveled home.

Then he asked the Lord to bless Reuben and make him a blessing to many.

This man is not quoting a prayer. He is praying from his heart like King David did, like Moses and all the ancient patriarchs prayed. When did my people stop praying from their hearts and begin quoting prayers? I must learn to pray from my heart too.

"Ow! Ow! Ow!" Reuben limped as his bare feet stepped on one stone after another. "That hurts!" Then he began to laugh and dance around but that only added to the pain. "I can feel again." Cautiously he began to watch for pebbles as he walked along the well-packed road. His parents lived in a village a half-day's journey away so he had a lot of time to think about that awful day when leprosy suddenly appeared and made him an outcast.

His mother and father had both cried as they gave him a bowl and sent him away. It was the first time he had seen his father cry and all because Reuben woke up with white patches on his arms and blotches on his face. The Law said he had to leave his home and his village.

That first night he sat by the side of the road, unable to stop the tears of anger and hatred of The Law that had put him in this place. The only thing he knew about leprosy was that it was to be feared. An old man sat nearby, his face twisted, his nose, fingers and toes half gone.

"Sit here. If someone comes near, you must cover your mouth and yell, 'Unclean! Unclean!'"

Reuben could smell the man from a distance, but his voice was kind and comforting. For a week Reuben sat beside the old man, crying himself to sleep every night. Every day his sobbing mother left food on the ground nearby for him, always wrapped in a big leaf so no dishes had to be destroyed. The day he turned twelve both his parents came with tears streaming down their faces.

I am a dead man in their sight. My father will never see me become a bar mitzvah, a Son of the Covenant. I will never be called to read from the Torah. When they were gone he put his head down on his arms and sobbed. That was the last time he saw his parents.

✡ ✡ ✡

"I AM AN OLD MAN and I will die soon, God willing," the old man had said to him the next day. "But you are young. You can never go back to your family. Go to Jerusalem. It is a big city and people will give you alms. Perhaps you can find a place to beg where people are generous. You can't expect your mother to come out here crying every day. Leave! Give her some peace."

"How long do I have to stay there?" Reuben questioned.

"Until you die."

Chapter 3

I WONDER IF THE OLD MAN is still begging by the road. It's been years since I sat there beside him. I think perhaps he died, I hope he died. I wonder if my mother will cry when she sees me again or if she ever stopped crying. This is all so confusing. I was declared clean but I still can't hug my family or go into my parent's house.

Reuben looked again in amazement at his fingers. Yesterday they were only half there, today they were like new. Sometimes people had paid him with food to pull cooked eggs out of the hot coals for them and he could do it because he couldn't feel any pain as his flesh burned. He opened and closed his hands remembering how hard it was to pick up coins when people threw them into the dirt beside him. His toes too had been half gone. Again he counted ten fingers and ten toes. He began to jog down the road chanting.

"Ten fingers! Ten toes! Ten Laws of Moses written on stone." He tried to recite every ten he could remember from his few years at *bet hasefer,* 'the house of the book'.

Ten men, a minion, are required for congregational prayers. God told Abraham he would save Sodom and Gomorrah if there were ten righteous men in the city.

"Ten, ten, ten," he chanted waving his hands in front of his face, thinking of all this time he had not studied or learned anything new. *I have lived more than sixteen years but in knowledge I am still eleven-year's-old.*

He almost ran down every incline and excitement overshadowed every steep climb along the way. He began to remember things from his childhood: the laughter as he played with his brothers; his mother's loving touch as she rubbed olive oil on a skinned knee; the patience of his father when Reuben crowded near to him, watching him make a sandal. He had not allowed himself to remember those things for years because of the pain it brought to his heart. But now he was going home. His heart almost exploded with joy.

It was dark when he crept near his family's home. Refusing to waken his family, he pulled his rags around him, like he had every night in Jerusalem, curled up on the ground and tried to go to sleep. Excitement kept him awake for a long time, but eventually his eyes closed and he slept.

The singing of birds woke him early in the morning. He never heard birds singing in the city and he had forgotten the chorus of sounds they made. He jumped up and standing a little distance from the house he cupped his hands around his mouth like he had done so often to yell, "Unclean!" But today he had a different message.

"Mama! Papa! Wake up! It's me, Reuben."

"Reuben? Is it you?" His mother stopped at the door and stared at him. "Why have you come back here? You are so tall. Why are you bald?"

"The leprosy is all gone," Reuben stated, "but I have to stay away from everyone for seven more days before the priest says I'm clean."

By then his father, two brothers and his sister, Deborah, had come crowding to the door too. Reuben wished he could hug them all, but he had to wait. Only The Law that had declared him unclean could declare him clean and let him live at home again.

Reuben found a place to sit nearby and all day his family hovered nearby talking to him, telling him about things that had happened there in the village. Deborah, two years older than Reuben told him she was betrothed and was so glad he would be home for her marriage the following year. His brother, Perez, was a year younger than Reuben and he was learning a trade.

"Judah, go and get your brother some better clothes," his mother called out and Reuben watched a boy run into the house. *So that's Judah. I didn't recognize him. He was only eight the last time I was home and now he's at the age when he too can become a Son of the Covenant.* Reuben looked down at the tattered clothing that barely covered his knees as the lad returned with a pile of linen garments, topped with a pair of new soft sandals of braided grass. Reuben picked up the sandals and glanced at his father.

The returning nod told him his father had made them with his own hands.

Every day the family brought food to him and left it nearby. One by one they sat and talked with him, telling him how they had grieved when he left.

While his brothers were off playing he told his parents about the prophet who was doing miracles all over Judea and how he had touched him. His mother cried when he told her that Jesus was the first person who had touched him since he left home. He explained the ritual the priest performed for his cleansing and how he washed himself and his clothes and a man helped to shave him.

"On the seventh day I have to return to the temple to wash my clothes, shave off my hair, immerse myself again," Reuben informed them, "and on the eighth day I need a lamb for an offering, and some flour and oil and two more turtledoves to take to the temple."

"Where did you get the birds and the cedar, scarlet and hyssop when you went to the temple the first time?" His father asked. Reuben told them about Tirus and the inn where he had begged. But he didn't tell them about his disappearing fingers and toes, how he smelled, or how often he was cold and hungry. His mother had cried enough. Instead he told them about Ethan and Judith, a couple from Bethlehem, who set up their booth by the inn and sold robes and blankets that Judith had woven.

"I am more than sixteen now, past the age to receive Papa's blessing, to take my place as a man and be called up to the Torah and read in the synagogue. When the priest declares me clean, Papa can take me, his first-born son to the synagogue and bless me."

With a proud gleam in his eye his father nodded his head. Reuben realized he wasn't the only one who had grieved about that missing blessing. But now it would come.

As the days passed he could tell by his parent's whispered conversations and the many errands that took his father away that they were working on providing for his trip back to the temple. Wealthy people would be asked to bring two male lambs and one ewe but his family was not wealthy. His father earned a living for the family making sandals so Reuben was required only to bring one lamb. Reuben was surprised and excited when his father said he would go with him. He wouldn't have to make the long walk to Jerusalem and back alone.

THE MORNING OF THEIR TRIP his father gave him another pair of new sandals he had made with palm bark soles and leather straps. *I won't have to worry about stepping on stones and hurting my feet today.* As they set off early in the morning on that seventh day his father carried food for their journey in the linen bag over his shoulder along with the flour and oil for the sacrifice.

On the way home my father will put his arm around me and when we get home again I will hug everyone in the family.

Reuben asked a million questions as he walked with his father and gradually learned all the news he had missed in the past years. The sun grew hot overhead. Sitting on the shady steps of the inn Reuben had seldom been in the sun. With his crippled hands and feet, it was difficult for him to move anywhere else. So he was surprised when his father draped a light shawl over him to protect his bare head from the hot sun.

Everything looked different to Reuben as they approached the city from the east. He could see the temple towering above the rest of the buildings as they trudged up through the Kidron Valley. They had walked at a good pace and were in the city in time for Reuben to make his appearance at the temple before the gates were closed.

Reuben's head moved from side to side, trying to see all the interesting sites. Today his father led him right into The Prayer Chamber, the huge open court he had seen before. Priests were carrying wood out of a room in the corner. He saw people throwing money into trumpet shaped containers. *That must be where people put their offerings. I wish I had some money to put into one of them. Maybe I'll be able to do that someday.* Quickly he counted them. Thirteen boxes shaped so the money could drop in but couldn't be taken out again.

"This is the Leper's Chamber," his father stated as he stopped by the door of a small room in a corner of this vast area. Reuben cautiously entered the chamber, trying to remember everything the priest had rattled off. This smaller, open courtyard was empty except for a *miqva,* an immersion pool cut out of the bedrock, completely lined with gray plaster and by law containing only fresh water. Reuben remembered the *miqva* in the village where he grew up, where people went to cleanse themselves. Reuben knew what to do but he was surprised when he noticed his father had followed him in.

"I will help you shave," his father stated. Reuben quickly immersed himself three times in the water making sure every part of him was submerged and then his father shaved off the bits of hair that had grown back during the week, only the razor gently touching his skin.

As they left the temple Reuben wondered where they would spend the night since he still couldn't stay at the inn. *Maybe my father will stay at the inn and I can sleep on the steps like I did before.* But together they wandered past the market stalls built into the street level of the Temple Mount. This time no one yelled at Reuben when he ran his hand over the soft wool or touched a silk garment. He looked like an ordinary person, his clothes were clean and his father was there to protect him.

None of these people know the wonderful miracle that has taken place in my life. Perhaps they have not even seen or heard about the prophet from Nazareth.

He followed his father through the Gate of the Essenes and down into the Hinnon Valley. Suddenly his father veered off the path and began to walk up a rocky hillside.

"Where are we going? There are no houses up there where you can stay."

"On a rocky hill like this there should be a cave or two, or maybe a cleft in the rocks. We can sleep under the stars tonight like the shepherds do."

Reuben had forgotten how wise his father was and it was proved when they soon found an overhang on the side of the hill. It was just the right size for them to fit in without touching one another. *I will be so glad when the priest says I am clean tomorrow and my father can touch me again. I think he wants to. I can see it in his eyes, but he will not despise the law and break its commands.*

Seated together on the ground, his father sang *motzi* before they ate grapes, cheese and barley loaves, saving two loaves for the morning. Reuben was tired but his mind was wide awake, thinking about what would happen the next day but gradually he drifted off to sleep dreaming about the lamb that would die for his cleansing.

Once again he heard birds singing. He was crouched on the steps of the inn and wanted to stay there with his eyes closed as long as he could. Then the sound of the birds reminded him where he was. He was healed and was on the hillside with his father.

His eyes popped open and fear gripped him when he realized his father wasn't there under the overhang.

Chapter 4

REUBEN STEPPED OUT OF THE CAVE and was relieved when he spotted his father walking on the hill. He watched him for a few seconds and then he remembered; his father was reciting *broche,* the short prayer of praise that was said every morning. Reuben tried to remember the words but four solitary years had erased the words from his memory. Tears welled up in his eyes as he thought of all the things he had forgotten. No one had spoken to him in all those months except to scold him, or tell him to get out of the way. No one had told him that he should still keep the law, even if he was a leper waiting to die.

His father returned and they ate the remaining barley loaves and hurried back into the city to the temple.

"Wait here," his father stated and disappeared down a flight of stairs. Reuben knew he was going for his own ritual cleansing so he would be purified to enter the Court of the Israelites. When he returned his head was wet. Reuben followed his father to where the merchants sold birds and animals and other items for temple sacrifices. The birds were quickly purchased but his father took a long time looking at the lambs.

Reuben stared at the one his father finally picked out and paid for. He slipped a short rope around its neck. Reuben wanted to run and throw his arms around it and pet it, but it was destined to die, just as he had been only a week before.

That lamb will die but I won't because Jesus touched me. I have to touch the lamb. Slowly he knelt down and put his arms around its neck and whispered it its ear. *Thank you!* Then he stood up ready to enter another part of the temple where he had never been before. His father indicated that Reuben should pick up the lamb and carry it.

With mixed feelings he proudly walked beside his father through the Outer Courtyard, and realized that his father knew exactly where to go. *My father has probably been to the temple here in Jerusalem many times and didn't know I was begging on the steps of the inn.* This time they went into and all the way through the Court of Prayer towards a half-circle flight of stairs. Reuben counted the uneven stone steps as they climbed. Fifteen!

"What do those signs say?" Reuben whispered pointing to several signs written in Greek and Latin.

"It says no Gentile can enter here or he will be put to death." At the top of the steps there was a set of bronze gates larger and more elaborate than any Reuben had seen before. "This is the Nicanor Gate," his father whispered to him. "It leads into the Court of Israelites and beyond that is the Court of Priests."

Reuben's eyes grew large as they entered the Court of the Israelites because ahead of them he could see smoke rising from the huge stone altar. It was a busy place. Priests hurried in with wood for the altar fire. Other priests were washing their hands and feet at a laver of water before they ascended the ramp to a ledge that ran all around the altar. Priests stood on that ledge placing offerings on the fire as smoke billowed up towards the open sky above. Reuben tried to look at everything at once. The white robes of some of the priests were blood-spattered and the entire area was saturated with the rising scent of meat searing on the altar.

Reuben and his father approached the low railing that separated the two areas and a priest came to meet them. When he learned that the lamb was Reuben's trespass offering he put his hands under Reuben's hands and together they lifted the lamb, moving it forward and backward and from side to side as a wave offering to the Lord. The priest took the lamb, the oil and the flour and walked away but indicated that Reuben and his father were to wait there.

Reuben kept his eye on his lamb as it was taken to the north side of the altar where animals designated for sacrifice were tied to rings secured into the floor. He grimaced as a priest slit its throat. One priest caught some of the blood in a bowl while another priest caught some of the blood in his bare hands. The blood caught in the bowl was thrown against the altar but Reuben was startled when the other priest approached him carrying the blood in his cupped hands. He dabbed blood from his hand on Reuben's right ear lobe, his right thumb and his right big toe. It suddenly became very significant to him, that today he had an ear lobe, a big toe and a thumb for the priest to anoint. Only a week before those things were missing.

The priest poured some of the oil into his left hand, sprinkled oil seven times towards the Holy of Holies and then came back to Reuben. With his right finger he dabbed oil on top of the blood on his earlobe, thumb and big toe. The rest of the oil he poured on top of Reuben's head to make atonement for him.

Reuben watched closely as the cut-up parts of his lamb were salted and placed on the altar to burn for a trespass offering. His two turtledoves were offered, one for a sin offering, the other for a burnt offering along with a handful of the flour for a meal offering. Finally the priest spoke the words Reuben had been waiting to hear.

"You are clean!"

Together he and his father left the Israelites Court, back down the fifteen steps, through the Court of the Women, the Outer Courtyard and out the gate. It seemed as if his father was in a hurry, his shoulders hunched, as they went down the huge stairway to the street but suddenly his father turned and drew Reuben into his arms as sobs rolled out of the very depths of his being. Reuben hugged him tight. How he had longed for this and it had taken the death of three birds and an innocent lamb to finally declare him cleansed.

ON THE WAY HOME Reuben and his father discussed the rite of passage Reuben had missed when he turned thirteen because of the leprosy.

"When we get home I will help you prepare and we will make arrangements for your Bar Mitzvah, when you will read from the Torah for the first time at synagogue."

"I want to learn again to say *broche*," Reuben stated emphatically. So his father taught him the words again as they walked along the road.

The journey home seemed to go faster than when they went into the city. As they neared their home his father gave a joyful yell and the whole family rushed to greet them. Reuben was crushed in his mother's arms while his brothers and sister laughed and pulled on him. Deborah couldn't resist running her hand over his shaved head, laughing at the soft bristles.

"Today I bestow on you a father's blessing," Reuben's father stated. "Our ancestor Isaac blessed Jacob and he became a great patriarch. Jacob in turn pronounced a blessing on every one of his twelve sons. Today, I give you my blessing. Today you are a man according to the Law. You can go into the Court of the Israelites and even be part of a quorum. You are alive again, my son. I bless you."

Yes, I am alive again.

The days passed with Reuben basking in family meals just like it used to be, except now everyone was older. His father sang the blessing at meals like he remembered and spent time helping Reuben learn the passage of Torah he would read on the following Sabbath, the story of Joshua sending ten spies to check out the land of Canaan.

He sent out ten spies. Reuben looked at his ten fingers.

"I was so happy to have ten fingers and ten toes again," Reuben told his father. "All the way home I tried to think of every ten I could remember. I forgot about the ten spies." He went on reading from the Torah, not noticing the look of distress on his father's face.

Reuben wasn't as excited when he read about the awful report eight of the spies brought back and how the people refused to move forward and win the land.

"So the Lord punished the people because of their lack of faith?"

"Yes, and for forty years they wandered around in the wilderness until that generation had all died and then he allowed their children to go into the land."

Reuben felt his father's pride as the family went to the synagogue. He watched and listened to everything that went on; from the moment the Torah was taken out of the Ark and carried around the room, to the moment it was returned to its symbolic resting place on the reading stand. Reuben had never in his life felt such fulfillment as he was called up to read from the Torah, the passage his father had helped him study. Reuben looked forward to the special celebration meal his mother had prepared at home but the rabbi approached them before they went out the door.

"You have not been here for a long time," the Rabbi stated, looking at Reuben. "Where have you been?"

"I went to Jerusalem because I had leprosy. But the Messiah healed me. See, I have no more leprosy." Reuben held out his hands and turned them over and over. He felt his father's hand heavy on his shoulder as the rabbi asked about the Messiah.

"Jesus of Nazareth. He touched me and I was healed." Reuben was shocked as the Rabbi gasped and his face contorted in rage.

"Blasphemy! Leave the synagogue. You are not allowed in this place again." Looking at Reuben's father he said, "Send him away. Do not associate with him any more. He is as good as dead to us."

It was happening all over again. He wasn't even allowed to wait until the Sabbath was over or to eat the special meal prepared for him. Within an hour everyone in the little village knew that Reuben had been put out of the synagogue. He had no choice but to leave town, which was what the law demanded. He walked a Sabbath-day's journey before he sat by the side of the road wondering what he should do. He couldn't cry 'unclean' and expect people to give him food.

After dark his sister crept near and gave him some of the food he would have eaten with his family and pressed a small moneybag into his hand. The next day he trudged back to the city with a huge ache in his heart.

prophet. From then on he was always sitting quietly nearby, listening and learning about the amazing man who had healed him. Reuben loved hearing what people had to say about Jesus.

FINALLY REUBEN REALIZED he had spent all his money. The only person he knew in all of Jerusalem was Tirus, the innkeeper. Slowly, he made his way back to the inn. Maybe Tirus would again feed him in exchange for odd jobs.

Reuben was glad to see the stall set up in front of the inn. Although it wasn't one of their High Holy Days, many people still came to the city to celebrate Rosh Hashanah. The last time he had seen this couple, the woman, Judith, had been in so much pain it was difficult for her to work. Today she was busy laying out the robes and blankets she had woven since the last time they had been here. For the first time, he could now talk to them and thank them for their kindness to him. When Judith dropped an article Reuben leapt forward to pick it up. He tugged on her sleeve.

"You dropped this," he said, placing the robe in her hands.

"Thank you." She turned and put the robe back on the pile.

"You have no son, no?" Reuben said softly and then pulled back when Judith turned swiftly, with an indignant expression on her face. Her expression changed again in an instant.

"No, I have no son," she replied sadly. "Do you live here in Jerusalem? What's your name?"

"My name is Reuben. I used to beg here beside the inn. I had leprosy, but Jesus healed me." He stood still as Judith looked into his eyes.

"I am to believe that you, such a beautiful lad, are the one we saw here? But you were so small." She stared at him for several minutes, scanning him from head to toe. Her eye widened when she saw the little bit of curly fuzz growing on his head. Reuben knew exactly when she realized he had been to the temple and gone through the cleansing ceremony. *When I was a leper crouched on the steps I seemed small. Now I am almost as tall as Judith.*

"How wonderful! Ethan! Come! This young man is Reuben, the leper who used to beg here by the inn. Jesus healed him." Reuben's heart flooded with joy when Judith reached out and took his hands in her own. She looked at his perfect toes sticking out of his sandals. Her fingers were soft as she ran them over his ears and touched his nose as if only by touching could she believe what she saw.

"Tirus told us you went back home to your family," Ethan said. "Your parents were overjoyed to see you, yes? Are they here with you?"

"They don't want me any more," Reuben replied and dipped his head to hide the sudden moisture in his eyes.

"Surely the priest has seen you and declared you clean. Does that make no difference to them?" Ethan questioned.

"The priest declared me clean and I went home. But when we went to the synagogue everyone wanted to know how it was that my leprosy was gone. I told them Jesus of Nazareth, the Messiah, touched me and healed me. Now I have been banished from the synagogue and banished from my home again. My parents had to say, I am as one dead to them. Do you need a son?" He saw the startled glance that flew between husband and wife.

Chapter 6

"I CAN WORK. My fingers are all here. I can do good work." Reuben knew they needed help. Judith had been in pain for a long time. *I wish she would seek out Jesus and be healed too.*

"Yes, come, you can help us with our work," Ethan finally stated, draping an arm over Reuben's shoulder as he gave him instructions.

Reuben was soon busy folding garments, making neat piles on the table just the way he had often seen Ethan and Judith do it. Only now, he wasn't watching from the steps of the inn. Now he was in the booth, his very own hands smoothing the garments and every now and then giving into the urge to bunch one up and hide his face in its softness. In all the time he had watched them he had never imagined what Judith's woven articles would feel like.

He loved working in the stall refolding articles after people had looked at them and tossed them carelessly back onto the pile. One. Two. Three. Four. He counted the robes in each pile. The blankets he piled in stacks of three, until everything was lined up neatly.

All the time he worked he listened. He tried to hide his excitement the day Judith finally decided to seek out Jesus for healing.

"Didn't you hear?" Someone sneered when Ethan asked about him. "He's afraid of the Pharisees. He isn't coming to the city."

Reuben turned away in disappointment.

The following days were busy, yet they seemed to drag. When would Jesus come back to the city? Reuben helped customers tie purchases onto their animals, his fingers agile, even with knots he had almost forgotten. At night he chose to curl up in his usual spot by the inn.

"It is where I'm used to sleeping," he told them, "keeping watch over your booth. When it looked like thieves were near I would crawl close to the booth and cry out. They would run away, afraid of my leprosy. You are kind people. You always put your coins into my bowl instead of throwing them on the ground. Watching your booth was something I could do for you."

✡ ✡ ✡

"I KNEW JESUS COULD DO IT." Reuben was ecstatic the day Judith came running back to the booth healed. He danced in circles around the stall. "Jesus can do anything! He's the Messiah, yes?" He saw Judith pause with a distant look in her eye.

"Careful who you say that to," Ethan advised him, a hand on Reuben's shoulder to calm him down. "You don't want to offend our Jewish leaders. They could make trouble for you."

"What can they do to me? They have already put me out of the synagogue, me, a Son of the Covenant. My parents don't want me. What more could they do?"

"Just be careful," Ethan repeated.

Reuben was so excited he had a hard time going to sleep that night. Silently he lay on the steps, praising God for Judith's healing. The next day the festival came to an end with the blowing of the Ram's Horn.

"May the final verdict be favorable," people called in greeting to one another as they left the city to go back to their homes. Reuben was sad to see this loving couple fold up their booth and leave. He would miss them but now he would be a helper to Tirus, running errands and sweeping in front of the inn and for that, Tirus would feed him.

"I have been apart from the law for a long time," Reuben stated. "For more than four years I have not been to synagogue to hear the reading of the Torah and I have not attended *bet hasfer.* I would like to go to the temple for prayer. When I was eleven, almost twelve, I ceased learning. I have lived more than sixteen years now and I have much to catch up on."

"Go! Every day you must go to the temple. Do your work before you go and after you come back." Tirus quickly laid down a schedule for him, working in the early mornings and evenings with the entire day free to catch up on what he had missed. He investigated the city now and then but it was the temple that fascinated Reuben.

One day he sat on a hill and just watched hundreds of people come and go, some climbing the numerous stones steps on the south side of the temple, every other step a bit wider to encourage people to meditate and pray as they walked up. It didn't take him long to recognize the difference in the gates and realize that people entered a double gate and came back out a triple gate. Maybe that was because everyone seemed to come back out at the same time, after the time of prayer.

On the day Reuben walked down into the Kidron Valley and sat on the opposite hill, he realized The Feast of Tabernacles, was nearing. People all over the city were gathering bundles of willows or cedars and building booths on top of their houses, in the courtyards and city squares. Each family would live for the seven days of the festival in their booth. *I wish I had a family to celebrate with.* But Reuben was content just to be in Jerusalem on such an occasion.

He walked through the outer courts of the Temple Mount, brave enough now to enter the Court of Prayer where crowds of people were always milling about.

He paused as he overheard a large group in Solomon's Porch, discussing Jesus of Nazareth. Slowly he edged closer to hear their conversation. People of all ages mingled together and their speech indicated they were all devout followers of the prophet.

"Shalom!"

Reuben was startled to find a boy about his own age standing beside him.

"You have heard about Jesus of Nazareth?" The boy asked.

"Yes, he healed me of leprosy and I would love to see him again and thank him."

"My name is Andrew. I'm here with my parents and my two sisters. We live here in Jerusalem and have just finished building our booth for the festival."

"I'm Reuben. I don't have a family anymore. I work at the inn, for Tirus but I don't think he has a booth."

"Why don't you come and stay with us in ours. My mother and my sister, Yakira, have been baking both fruit and vegetable *kugal* for days. Come and meet my family."

Reuben followed Andrew to where a small group stood apart from the others.

"This is Reuben. He has no family here in the city. Can he come and stay with us in our booth during the festival. He is one Jesus healed."

Within minutes the family had welcomed Reuben into their midst. Yakira appeared to be about a year younger than Reuben and her sister, Sheera, looked about thirteen. *She is almost the same age as my brother Judah.*

Andrew accompanied him back to the inn to tell Tirus their plans and for the next seven days of the feast he reversed his schedule. Early every morning Reuben ran back to the inn to do chores for Tirus after sleeping with the family in the small wooden structure. Reuben was so happy to be in the midst of a family again, in a booth during this celebration to remember how their ancestors lived for forty years in the wilderness.

"For more than four years I was here in Jerusalem, sitting in front of the inn begging. So I haven't seen much of the city or the Temple," Reuben whispered to his new friend, Andrew.

"I will show you the city," Andrew stated. And he did. They spent the day wandering around. He pointed out the Roman barracks and storehouses, which were not too far from the Temple Mount, and the town hall just west of the first city wall ever built.

"That's the theater." Andrew pointed to the huge walled amphitheater as they passed it. "King David's tomb is just a bit farther. Look! There's the tomb!" Andrew broke into a run with Reuben close on his heels.

Reuben was in awe. He was gazing on the tomb of their most famous king. He thought of all the wonderful stories he remembered about King David but Andrew, told stories about King David that Reuben had never heard.

"Jesus is in the city for the Feast of Tabernacles," Andrew's father informed them early one morning. "We must watch for him at the temple."

When the Sabbath arrived, during the festival, Reuben went with Andrew's family again to the synagogue to hear the reading of the Torah. This day, the reading included the story of God calling Moses to lead the Children of Israel out of Egypt. One portion of the reading stuck in Reuben's mind.

"The Lord said to Moses, 'I am making a covenant with you in the presence of all your people. I will perform miracles that have never been performed anywhere in all the earth or in any nation. And all the people around you will see the power of the Lord-the awesome power I will display for you. But listen carefully to everything I command you today. I will go ahead of you and drive out the Amorites, Canaanites, Hittites, Perizzites, Hivites and Jebusites.'"

The Jebusites were living right here when King David conquered Jerusalem. Jehovah kept the promise He made to Moses and drove out the Jebusites for David.

The family had no sooner left the synagogue than they began to hear rumours and whispers that the Jewish authorities were looking for Jesus because again he had healed a man on the Sabbath, this time a man who had been born blind.

"The man's parents were questioned over and over," a man nearby told anyone who would listen. "They had no idea what had happened. But the Pharisees were angry because the Nazarene made mud and put it on the man's eyes. Working on the Sabbath made them furious."

Reuben and Andrew heard some people quietly talking about what a good man Jesus was. But other people were open in their ridicule.

"He is just fooling people," they scoffed.

"What about what one man said to our Jewish leaders? He said, since the world began, no one has been able to open the eyes of someone born blind. If this man were not from God he couldn't have done it." That was followed by another flurry of debate.

"Do you think Jesus is the Messiah? This could be one of the miracles Jehovah told Moses about." Reuben whispered to Andrew.

"I do believe." Andrew whispered back. "Papa says I'm to be careful that no one hears me say that but who else could do so many miracles?"

Half way through the festival they heard that Jesus was teaching in the temple again. The boys rushed to the temple and were just in time to hear Jesus speak. Reuben didn't know much about sheep so he listened closely to what the prophet was saying about them. He tucked even more things away in his mind.

"I tell you the truth. I am the good shepherd. I sacrifice my life for the sheep. No one can take my life from me. I sacrifice it voluntarily for I have the authority to lay it down when I want to and also to take it up again."

Reuben and Andrew talked about the things Jesus had said, but neither of them knew anything about sheep so it didn't make much sense to them.

"What I teach is not my own teaching but it comes from God who sent me. Whoever is willing to do what God wants will know whether what I teach comes from God or if I speak on my own authority. I perform one miracle on the Sabbath and you are all surprised. Yet you circumcise your son on the eighth day even if it falls on a Sabbath. Why are you angry with me because I made a man well on the Sabbath?"

Within minutes people were arguing loudly about whether Jesus could possibly be the Messiah or not.

"Messiah will be a descendant of King David and will be born in Bethlehem." Reuben heard a man state vehemently. "We all know this man is from Galilee."

Reuben remembered the man who prayed for him by the Serpents Pool he began to wonder if he could pray like that, to the God of Abraham, Isaac and Jacob. *I am a Son of the Covenant. Maybe he would hear me.*

"God of Israel," he whispered. "I give you praise. I pray that you would bless me. I am alone and I need a family. You are the God of miracles. Please help me."

Reuben went back to stay with Tirus after the festival was over, but every Sabbath he joined Andrew and his family at their synagogue. *I wonder if Andrew's family would like another son.*

"Tirus! They're back." Reuben could hardly contain himself the day Judith and Ethan returned to the city many weeks later. He wanted to do everything for them, unload the donkey and set up the booth. Tirus came to the door of the inn, a wide smile on his face as he watched the three of them.

"I have brought you something," Judith said to Reuben when everything was in place and she and Ethan were ready to retire to a room in the inn.

Reuben was stunned when she handed him a new robe, made of the softest wool he had ever felt.

"For me?" The couple smiled while Reuben put the robe on over his linen garment. It was a perfect fit. "This will keep me warm at night," Reuben stated as he pulled the robe about him and settled down on the steps of the inn. The next day Reuben was everywhere at once. He could not seem to keep his hands off the robes and blankets.

Business was brisk with thousands of people that had come to the city for Passover but Reuben suddenly noticed a family that looked familiar coming along the street. It was Andrew and his entire family. With pride, Reuben introduced Ethan and Judith to them when they stopped at the booth. Reuben told about spending time with Andrew's family in the booth they erected for the Feast of Tabernacles and the wonderful *kugel* Yakira had made for them to eat.

"We're just on our way to watch the high priest bring the chosen Pascal lamb into the city," Andrew's father informed them. "The lamb will be tied at the temple so people can see it and assure themselves that it has no blemishes." As the family left they invited Ethan, Judith and Reuben to join them at their synagogue the following Sabbath.

They hadn't been gone long when a commotion could be heard above the normal mingling crowd, the sound of people singing and yelling in glee.

"I wonder what's going on. Perhaps it's the high priest bringing the Pascal lamb into the city. Should I run and see?" Judith moved from behind the stall.

"We'll stay here." Ethan nodded his consent. Reuben continued to help Ethan in the stall, all the time hearing a celebration going on somewhere else in the city.

A short time later Judith stumbled back to the stall. Clutching her robe close around her, she staggered and almost fell before Ethan grabbed her shaking hands and sat her down.

Reuben backed away when he saw her frightened, tear-streaked-face. Slowly he moved outside the stall, giving them privacy, but he stayed close by. Then his own brow wrinkled in confusion as he overheard what Judith said.

"It was Jesus coming into the city. He is the one they call the King of the Jews. He was born in Bethlehem."

Reuben opened his mouth to ask her to describe this exciting procession when Judith began to sob and Ethan turned ashen white as he wrapped his arms around his wife.

I don't understand. How wonderful to see Jesus coming into the city. If he was born in Bethlehem, he surely is Messiah. Why is Judith so upset?

"That man," Judith spat out the words, "is the reason our son, Jair was killed."

Reuben pulled his robe close around himself and backed farther away at the venom in her voice. He had never seen Judith like this. Just then Ethan looked up and saw Reuben watching them.

"Reuben, go to Tirus. Tell him I sent you to stay with him." Reuben turned and scurried into the inn to find Tirus. *Messiah will be born in Bethlehem. Jesus was born in Bethlehem.* These thoughts tumbled and twisted together in Reuben's mind.

Chapter 7

REUBEN AVOIDED THE COUPLE during the days ahead. It broke his heart to see them suffering and one day Reuben felt so uncomfortable around Ethan and Judith that he finally wandered off into the city. Maybe he would see Jesus somewhere. Surely he would be in the city for this most sacred of festivals and the most likely place to find him would be at the temple.

When he arrived at the temple he hurried up the steps and into the outer courts where people gathered and teachers taught. He caught sight of Andrew and his family in the crowd and realized the reason for the crowd. Jesus was there. Finally he would be able to hear him teach again. There were many Greeks in the crowd by the looks of their clothing and hairstyles. Reuben moved closer so he could hear what was being said and Andrew came to sit down beside him.

"The man right beside Jesus is Peter, one of his disciples," Andrew said. Reuben could tell he was a man used to hard work, his face weather-beaten: various parts of him always in motion.

"The one on the other side is John." Andrew stopped talking as Jesus began to teach the crowd. Reuben glanced quickly at John, who stood quietly by, looking at peace, but listening to every word his teacher said.

"Unless a kernel of wheat is planted in the soil and dies, it remains alone. But its death will produce many new kernels, a beautiful harvest of new lives."

Reuben puzzled over this statement, but had to bury that thought for later as Jesus continued to speak.

"Should I pray, 'Father, save me from this hour?' But this is the very reason I came! Father, bring glory to your name."

Reuben cringed as a thunderous sound roared through the court.

"What was that? Was it thunder?" People everywhere asked in fear, puzzled at seeing the clear blue sky above. But people with keen ears had heard words in the midst of the thunder. Reuben heard the words. *I have already brought glory to my name and I will do so again.*

"The voice was for your benefit, not mine." Jesus stated. "The time for judging this world has come, when Satan, the ruler of this world, will be cast out. And when I am lifted up from the earth, I will draw everyone to myself."

People began asking questions and Reuben hoped he could remember the things he heard so later he could think about what they could possibly mean. The prophet's last statement stuck in his mind.

"Put your trust in the light while there is still time; then you will become children of the light."

Reuben glanced around him and when he looked back, Jesus had gone. He hardly slept that night as words and thoughts rolled around in his mind. Over and over he heard that strange voice. *I have already brought glory to my name and will do so again.* Every time he thought about that loud statement he shivered and the hair on his neck bristled. What did it mean and who said it? Finally in the wee hours of the morning he drifted off to sleep and woke a couple hours later groggy and tired.

He set off towards the temple hoping to find Jesus again but first he met Andrew on the street.

"Reuben, I didn't show you the Hippodrome yet. It's right here, close to the temple," Andrew stated, pointing to an enormous building.

Reuben was amazed at the huge arena that Herod had built for chariot racing.

"I've never noticed this huge place before, but I've always been excited about getting to the temple. Last year at Passover, I was a leper and had no part in the festivities. This year will be different. What takes place in the temple?"

"Every family chooses their Pascal lamb ahead of time. The one the high priest chose is already tied up at the temple so people can look at it and know it is a perfect lamb. There was a huge procession as he brought his chosen lamb into the city. Everyone was singing a Psalm, 'Blessed is he who comes in the name of the Lord.'"

"Did you know that Jesus came into the city riding on a donkey the same day? My friend Judith went to see and the people were singing the same thing."

Reuben and Andrew were quiet as they pondered that.

"Do you think Jesus is in the temple? I hope we see him. Tell me what else will happen." Andrew carried on with his explanation as they continued on towards the temple.

"It is exciting and amazing. Last year I went with my father to take our lamb to the temple. On the day of preparation thousands and thousands of families will bring their lambs to the temple. Trumpets blow and the Levites and the people all sing the Hallel Psalms.

"There aren't that many families in Jerusalem. Are there?"

"No but a lot of people are camped outside the city walls. As long as they are within a Sabbath Day's journey, about 3000 steps, the distance we are allowed to walk on the Sabbath, they can come to the temple."

"How will they ever be able to sacrifice that many lambs?"

"All the priests have been called to Jerusalem to help, so hundreds of priests will be on duty. The people are divided into three groups. The first group enters the Court of the Priests and the doors are closed. The head of each family kills their own lamb. Priests with bowls work together in pairs. One catches the blood in a bowl, and exchanges it for an empty bowl and moves to the next family in line. The priest who took the bowl of blood passes it to yet another priest who throws the blood against the altar and gives him back the empty bowl and by then the first priest already has the blood from the next lamb. On and on they go and by the end of the day you can't imagine the amount of blood that has been spilled."

"What happens to the slain lambs?"

"Every lamb has a sign around their neck giving the name of who owns it. After our lamb is killed a Levite takes it to the area where it is skinned. The fat is salted, put into a bowl and burned on the altar according to The Law. The remainder of the lamb is given back to our family to roast and eat at home for the Passover feast.

"My father tells about the time when they cleansed and rededicated the temple when Hezekiah was king. The people brought so many sacrifices and thanksgiving offerings to the Lord that there were not enough priests to do all the work. They had to call purified Levites to help them until all the offerings had been made."

✡ ✡ ✡

REUBEN AND ANDREW FOUND JESUS in plain view at Solomon's Porch, teaching the people. All the benches were occupied so, while Andrew went to find his family, Reuben made himself comfortable on the floor leaning against one of the huge pillars. He turned his whole attention to Jesus; the man was telling stories again and Reuben loved listening to his stories.

This was a story about a man who owned a vineyard and a winepress. He built a wall of protection around it and a watchtower. Then, he leased out the business and want away expecting to receive rent on an annual basis. When the harvest was in and the rent due, he sent his servants to collect his money, but the renters beat one servant, killed one of them and stoned another.

The owner then sent a larger group of servants to collect his rightful due, and the same thing happened again. Finally, he decided to send his son thinking certainly his son would receive respect from the renters. But instead, thinking that if they killed the son they could inherit it all themselves, the renters dragged him outside the vineyard and murdered him.

Reuben hoped to hear an end to the story, but instead, Jesus asked the religious leaders in the crowd what the owner would do when he came back himself.

"He will kill them and lease the vineyard to someone who will give him his share of the harvest."

Then Jesus quoted a portion of a psalm. "The stone that the builders rejected has now become the chief cornerstone. I tell you, the Kingdom of God will be taken away from you and given to a nation that will produce the proper fruit."

Reuben didn't understand what he meant by that but the religious rulers were furious. It almost seemed as though they were going to arrest Jesus but the people wanted to hear more, to talk to him and touch him. The leaders finally backed down, not wanting to displease the people.

Reuben was pleased when Jesus told another story about a man who prepared a huge wedding banquet, but all the people he invited refused to come. Then he sent his servants out in every direction to bring in anyone, the good and the bad until all the seats were filled.

I could have been invited to that banquet. With that thought in his mind and weary from a sleepless night, Reuben dozed off, dreaming about being in the home of a wealthy man, feasting on every sort of food imaginable.

He awoke with a start when Jesus, in a stern voice, started to criticize the religious leaders. Reuben had been taught to respect and revere these men but as he listened he began to understand what Jesus was saying. Those leaders really did like to be seen and heard, just like Jesus said, to have the best seats, and hear their money make a lot of noise as it fell down into the trumpet shaped treasury boxes. Fear shot through Reuben. What would happen to Jesus if their religious leaders became offended again?

REUBEN RETURNED TO THE TEMPLE the next day but didn't see Jesus. Nor did her see him on preparation day, the day before Passover. Then he heard awful news. Jesus had been arrested.

Here I am, finally old enough to go into the Court of the Israelites and the Sanhedrin is trying to get rid of our Messiah, before he even has a chance to liberate us from the Romans.

Reuben listened to all the gossip and hurried about to keep up with the events. The soldiers with their commanding officer and temple guards took Jesus before Annas, a very influential man, who was once the high priest and still carried the title. He was also the father-in-law of the current high priest. Reuben blended in with the crowd milling around outside the high priest's courtyard.

There's Peter, one of Jesus' followers, going into the courtyard. Reuben crouched down by the gate in the familiar beggar's position so he could watch, unnoticed, undisturbed. He saw the man join the household servants and guards as they huddled around a charcoal fire.

"You are one of his followers, aren't you?"

Reuben peeked out from under his robe and realized the woman was talking to Peter. He clapped his hand over his mouth to prevent a gasp escaping when he heard Peter lie and say he didn't even know Jesus.

When they brought Jesus out and took him to Caiaphas the high priest Reuben followed, fearing what would happen there because everyone knew that Caiaphas was the one who said, "Better for one man to die for the people." By now it was very early in the morning and Reuben had seen a steady stream of men slip quietly into the high priest's residence. Seeing how they were dressed, he recognized them as members of the Sanhedrin.

Now they will release him. These are the men who uphold the Law. Just this very year the Romans have taken away the right of the Sanhedrin put anyone to death.

"Where are they taking him?" Reuben asked someone nearby as they brought Jesus out of Caiaphas' court later, with his hands bound.

"They have condemned him for blasphemy and are taking him to Pilate to be tried."

Reuben's heart almost stopped when he heard that news. Pilate was a brutal man who had even recently killed Galilean Jews as they sacrificed at the temple. Reuben ran to catch up with the group as they neared Pilate's house. Pilate came out to see what they wanted because none of their nation could enter into Pilate's palace or they would be ritually unclean for the Passover.

"What is the charge against this man?" Pilate asked.

"We wouldn't have brought him to you if he weren't guilty," the crowd yelled.

"Then you take him and judge him by your own law."

"Only the Romans are permitted to execute someone," was the contemptuous reply. Reuben knew then, that his own people wanted to crucify Jesus, the man who had healed him, given him a life again. What could he do?

Pilate went back into his palace and they hauled Jesus inside to be questioned by him. Reuben looked around and was stunned by the hatred and anger flashing from the eyes, the clenched fists and the scowls on the faces of the men behind this awful situation.

He was greatly relieved when Pilate came out and said he found no guilt in the man and because he released one prisoner every year at Passover, he offered to make Jesus the prisoner he would release. He gave the people the choice between Jesus and Barabbas. Reuben relaxed and took a deep breath.

They will choose Jesus and he will be released. But by now the anger of the crowd had built to a frenzy. Reuben stared in disbelief when the crowd screamed for Barabbas to be set free.

Finally, Pilate brought Jesus out again, this time dressed in a purple robe, a crown of thorns gouging his scalp, rivulets of blood creeping down his face. Reuben's eyes filled with tears, his heart almost stopped beating and his breath became shallow and painful.

"Crucify him!" the crowd roared.

"Take him and crucify him yourselves," Pilate said. "I find no guilt in him."

"He calls himself the Son of God." Someone yelled.

Reuben saw Pilate's face turn white when he heard that statement and took Jesus back inside to talk to him again. The next time he brought him out and tried to release him the crowd went wild.

"You are no friend of Caesar's if you release him. Anyone who claims himself a king is a rebel against Caesar."

By this time it was noon and Pilate finally sat down on the judgment seat on the stone pavement.

"Here is your king." He stated.

"We have no king but Caesar. Crucify him!" Pilate finally turned Jesus over to the crowd and they took him away to crucify him.

If he is Messiah, certainly God will protect and deliver him.

Chapter 8

REUBEN SAT ON THE SIDE of the hill. The excitement of the presentation of the Pascal lambs in the Temple with all its music and celebration, that he had so longed to see, was totally forgotten as the man he had come to love was nailed to a cross, spit on and taunted. Glancing in fright around him, he was relieved to see young friends and others of The Way, people who had invited him into their homes and they looked as shocked as he was at what was taking place.

Then a sign was nailed to Jesus' cross, claiming him to be the King of the Jews. An image flashed through Reuben's mind of each Pascal Lamb with a sign around its neck telling whom the lamb belonged to. Across the way he caught sight of Ethan and Judith huddled together with expressions of hatred on their faces as they saw the sign. Tears poured down Reuben's face. He bent over, clutching his stomach as nausea boiled inside him. Once again, someone he loved was being ripped from his life.

Reuben shook with fright when the sky darkened and at the moment his beloved healer died, an earthquake shook the city. Reuben sat, quivering on the ground and suddenly realized it was the ninth hour and he had missed the sacrifice of the Passover Lamb. He sat, lonely and alone, staring at the lifeless body of the one he thought was the Messiah.

Finally one of the wealthy men Reuben had often seen climbing that impressive elite flight of stairs to enter the temple came and took the body of Jesus off the cross.

Reuben trudged his way back to the temple, hoping to find some solace there. But all he found was confusion, crying and wailing as the last of the people ran out of the temple. Reuben continued on right into the Court of the Israelites. He had to see what was left of the celebration. The floor was awash in blood, just like Andrew had told him, but agitated priests rushed around. Above the din Reuben heard awful, unbelievable news.

Further inside the temple, at the very entrance to their Holy of Holies, their beautiful curtain had been torn from top to bottom. Reuben quickly turned his eyes away from that scene of destruction.

No one but the High Priest can enter there and only once a year. What would happen to anyone that accidentally looked into that Most Holy Place? The Ark of the Covenant hasn't been in there for generations, but it's still our Most Holy Place. What has caused all these awful things to happen? There had been major damage in the temple. The huge lintel had broken, splintered and fallen and the beautiful room where the Sanhedrin met, the

Chamber of Hewn Stones, was so damaged the group had to meet elsewhere.

FINALLY REUBEN TRUDGED BACK to the inn, grief written all over his face. So many terrible things had happened in this one day. He didn't really want to see Ethan and Judith, but he didn't know where else to go. Tirus gave him something to eat and Reuben retreated to the place where he usually slept. At least the innkeeper was not glad Jesus had died, not like Ethan and Judith. Reuben listened as the three adults stood outside talking about what had happened.

"He was taken off the cross and buried before the High Sabbath but the chief priests and the Pharisees were still not satisfied. They asked Pilate to secure the tomb. So the tomb was sealed with his own signet and guards are keeping watch."

"What do they expect to happen?" Ethan questioned with an unfamiliar bit of sarcasm. "The man is dead. He might have raised Lazarus, but who is going to raise him? Do they think he can do that himself?"

ON THE FIRST DAY OF THE WEEK, with the High Sabbath over, thousands of people who had descended on the city for the celebration began to pack up and leave for their homes. With mixed emotions Reuben watched Ethan and Judith leave.

I wonder if I will ever see them again. But he had other things on his mind too. The body of Jesus was gone. The tomb was empty. Rumours were flying around. Some said his body had been stolen. Others said he was alive again.

Reuben had to know what happened. He wandered around the city listening for information. People were saying his disciples stole the body away. Other people were saying he was alive again just like Lazarus. Then he heard that several of Jesus' disciples had seen him alive. He went to the temple but couldn't find him. He didn't even see Andrew and his family there.

I'll go to the well. That's a good place to hear all the latest news. Before any women came to draw water, Reuben found a place nearby and sat with his arms wrapped around his knees, his head resting on his arms like a beggar, asleep. Then he listened.

"I heard that Mary went to the tomb. The body was gone but while an angel talked to her, suddenly that man, Jesus, was right there, talking to her. He wasn't dead after all."

He was dead. I watched him die. But now he's alive again? Reuben had a hard time sitting still. He was so excited he wanted to run somewhere and find Jesus but he remained still, hoping they'd say something else. But the conversation turned to problems the women were having at home and what their children were learning at *bet hasefer.* It seemed like forever before they finally filled their water jars and left.

Over the next few days Reuben helped Tirus but often his curiosity would take him off into the city again.

He took to visiting the temple almost every day and overheard many whispered conversations. People were afraid of the priests and Pharisees so no one dared speak out loud about what had happened. A week passed and finally he heard some exciting news, spoken in a loud whisper somewhere behind him.

"Jesus is going to meet with his disciples in Galilee. They are probably all there now."

When he heard that statement, Reuben determined that he too would go to Galilee. He had no idea where he would find the disciples, but he had to go. He wanted so much to see Jesus with his own eyes. He didn't want to spend the rest of his life wondering if he really was alive. He had to know.

When he told Tirus he was going to Galilee Tirus got a faraway look in his eyes. *He would like to go too.* But instead, Tirus packed enough food to last Reuben on the journey to Galilee. At the last minute, since he hadn't seen Andrew for a few days, Reuben decided to stop at his house to tell him where he was going.

"We heard too, that Jesus was going to be in Galilee," Andrew said excitedly. "Please, Papa, can I go with Reuben?"

Reuben could see that same longing look in the eyes of Andrew's parents. *They would like to go too.*

"Can I go along?" Yakira asked. "I can look after food for you along the way."

"Go, all three of you, with our blessings. Andrew, take care of your sister. And make sure you find a synagogue to attend on the Sabbath and be careful who you talk to and what you say. Not everyone believes as we do."

The trip to Galilee was nothing like his solitary trip back to his home village to see his parents. Yakira was full of energy, strolling along beside them, adding her own words as Andrew told Reuben things he had not heard.

"The grave clothes were still in the tomb," Andrew said.

"But the napkin from his face was folded and left," Yakira piped up, "just like we fold our napkin after we eat, to let Mama know we will be back for the next meal."

There were many people on the road, going both ways. Sometimes the trio walked with them. Sometimes they stayed just within earshot of other people to hear what they were discussing. Reuben had told his friends what had happened to him at the synagogue back home so they were careful not to talk about all the strange things that had happened unless the people brought up the subject.

"What did you hear about those things?" Reuben or Andrew would sometimes ask people as they walked along together and that would open a torrent of opinions. Some ranted about Jesus bringing them that close to having the Romans take away everything they had worked for, and they held up a finger and thumb with only a tiny space between them. Other times, the people would almost whisper their answers until they heard Reuben's story of being healed.

The journey from Jerusalem to Galilee took them three days. At night they joined other travellers who slept under the stars along the way. Yakira kept her word and pulled food from their supplies for each meal. It was wonderful for Reuben to have his two friends join him in reciting the morning prayers as the sun rose each day. The closer they got to Galilee, the more excited they became.

"How will we find the disciples?" Yakira finally asked, after they had been travelling beside the length of the Sea of Galilee for almost a full day. "I could ask at the well when women come to get water."

"If they are here, if Jesus is here, everyone will know and there will be a crowd," her brother replied. As they walked along they only had to listen to what people were talking about and soon they knew exactly where to go.

"I want to see Jesus and to know for certain he is alive again," Reuben stated emphatically. "I watched him die. I know he was dead and I grieved for him. Now I want to know the truth. Remember that day in the temple when a loud thundering voice said, 'I have been glorified and will be glorified again?' If Jesus is alive then God has been glorified again, just like the voice said."

"There's a crowd," Andrew pointed ahead to where a huge group of people had gathered. They rushed to mingle with the crowd and suddenly, through an opening in the throng of people, Reuben saw the prophet he had come to love. He was speechless. All he could do was to grab Andrew's arm and point ahead. Yakira saw him pointing and her face creased in a huge grin.

The excitement in the air could almost be touched. Reuben was relieved to see Peter alongside Jesus. The last time he saw Peter was when he lied about knowing Jesus. Reuben wondered what had transpired between the two men since then.

Suddenly Reuben comprehended all the unknown facts that had been twisting and turning in his mind. *Jesus, was dead and now he is alive. He really is our Messiah.*

They spent the day with the crowd in Galilee, thrilled to see that Jesus was not just there, but talking and eating with the people. The following morning the trio started home. The return trip was totally different. They were full of excitement; talking constantly of the things they would tell their parents and Tirus.

If Ethan and Judith return to the city, I can tell them that Jesus is alive again, that I saw him with my own eyes. That He really is the Messiah. But that doesn't change the fact that their baby was killed.

Chapter 9

IT WAS SEVERAL WEEKS before Reuben heard anything more about Jesus but he spent as much time as he could at the temple with other followers of The Way, meeting at Solomon's Porch, where people took turns explaining the things Jesus had taught them. They talked, not just about the facts and information, but of a new way to live. Things Reuben had heard but not understood.

"Now we understand what he meant about a temple being torn down and built again in three days. He was talking about his own body." The man who made that statement was excited about what he was learning. "That's what he meant too, about a kernel of wheat being put in the ground and dying, but then bringing forth much fruit."

When a couple reported that Jesus had told them that all the scriptures were about him, Reuben was puzzled but he listened carefully to what they said. He made sure he was at a synagogue every Sabbath and every time he heard the words of the Torah he understood more. It was like fresh water to his soul.

"Perhaps this is the time when Jesus will return the kingdom to Israel," a man whispered to his companions.

"What a great event that would be. He did tell us we would reign with him and sit on thrones," another man replied. "All His disciples are back here in Jerusalem, but no one knows where."

Reuben didn't expect to hear news like this and it made him think.

Then one day there was news of a different sort. Jesus was gone again but this time someone had seen him rise up into the clouds. Everyone was talking about it.

"He disappeared just like Elijah, except Elijah went up in a whirlwind."

"Two angels told his disciples he would come back the same way but with the sound of a trumpet."

Reuben hoped he would come back soon.

Days passed and the only time Reuben saw any of the disciples was at the temple at the hour of prayer. Rumours were that they were all together in a house; praying and waiting for a gift Jesus had promised to send them. Reuben couldn't imagine what the gift would be or how it would arrive, but he heard the disciples were to stay in Jerusalem until it came.

PEOPLE WERE FLOODING into Jerusalem again, this time for Shavuot, the fiftieth day after Passover, a celebration of when The Law was given to Moses. At midnight people began to bring their burnt offerings and peace offerings to the temple to be inspected before the morning sacrifice.

Reuben pictured in his mind the watchman high on the top of the temple, giving the signal when the morning glow extended as far as Mt. Hebron and then the day would begin. This was another one of the special days when the Levites chanted the Hallel, a single flute beginning and ending the song and the voices of children blending in with those of the men. He wondered if Jesus would come back when the ram's horn was blown.

As he walked to the synagogue Reuben looked at the throngs of people and tried to identify where they had come from. He heard Egyptian, Arabian, and Libyan dialects that he had learned to recognize during his years in front of the inn. Even people from Mesopotamia, Phrygia and Pamphylia had come to Jerusalem to celebrate Shavuot. They were all Israelites, descendants of Abraham and Moses, from all the places where their people had at one time or another been exiled and where they had remained. Perhaps the nice summer weather had something to do with that, but the most obvious fact was that they had returned to celebrate the day when God, with his own finger wrote his law in stone.

There was added pomp and ceremony in the synagogue as the Torah was taken from its special cupboard, called the Ark, and paraded around before being laid on the reading table. It had been a year since they read this passage so as it was read Reuben was in awe all over again. In his mind he pictured the roar of the thunder and the lightening as a thick cloud covered the mountain. He imagined the people trembling at a loud blast from a ram's horn and then Mount Sinai covered with smoke as the Lord descended on it in the form of fire. The blast of the ram's horn grew louder and louder as Moses spoke and God replied in thunder.

I wish God would come into our Holy of Holies again in a cloud of smoke. I wish the cloud would be so thick that the priests couldn't even carry on their work like it was when Solomon dedicated his temple. Reuben was deep in thought as he left the synagogue, thinking of Moses walking up the mountain, into the smoke. Back in the narrow streets of Jerusalem he saw envoys from synagogues as far away as Rome and Egypt who were bringing the temple tax from their synagogues. He could imagine what a great production that would be as the boxes of money were opened in the temple.

But the special part of the day was the presentation of the two 'wave' loaves, made from the very first bit of wheat that had been harvested, exactly the right amount weighed out to make two loaves. The loaves today were made with yeast and would be waved, just like the priest had helped him wave the lamb he brought for his cleansing. But today there would be several offerings, seven lambs, a young bull and two rams for the burnt offering, a young goat for the sin offering and two more lambs for the peace offering. Reuben didn't stay to watch it all but left the temple and bought a cheese blintz to eat. As he was enjoying his food, he heard a commotion not far away.

Walking towards the noise, munching on his food, he again recognized Israelites from many countries and the sound was like nothing Reuben had ever heard. It was as if every language was being spoken at once.

"We are Jews from every part of the earth yet we are all hearing these men speak the wonders of God in our own language," a man shouted in excitement.

Then Reuben recognized Peter, that disciple he heard tell a lie in the High Priest's courtyard. But he had also seen him with Jesus in Galilee. He listened closely as Peter began to speak.

"These men are not drunk," he explained. "God has poured out His Spirit as was spoken by the prophet Joel."

"Men of Israel, listen to this: Jesus of Nazareth was a man accredited by God to you by miracles, wonders and signs, which God did among you through him, as you yourselves know.

"This man was handed over to you by God's set purpose and foreknowledge; and you, with the help of wicked men, put him to death by nailing him to the cross. But God raised him from the dead, freeing him from the agony of death, because it was impossible for death to keep its hold on him. God has raised this Jesus to life, and we are all witnesses of the fact."

Reuben understood what the man was saying. *I saw Him too. I am a witness.*

"Exalted to the right hand of God, he has received from the Father the promised Holy Spirit and has poured out what you now see and hear. God has made this Jesus, whom you crucified, both Lord and Christ," Peter stated boldly. He looked from person to person, making eye contact with each one, almost challenging someone to disagree.

The Gift! This Holy Spirit Peter is talking about is the gift Jesus promised to give us. Reuben's heart felt like it would swell and burst right out of his body in his excitement. Glancing around at the crowd, Reuben was surprised to see Judith and Ethan. At that moment Judith looked right at him and her eyes widened in recognition. Reuben began to edge his way towards them. As he came close to them he heard Ethan speak quietly to his wife.

"It makes sense," Ethan whispered. "Judith, it does make sense. God sacrificed his own Son. That's why John, the Baptizer, called Him the Lamb of God, which takes away the sins of the world, God's human Passover lamb. Nothing could ever constitute as great a sacrifice or be acceptable to Jehovah."

Reuben gasped in delight. Finally Ethan understood. He was right. Jesus died at the ninth hour, the exact time when the Passover sacrifices ended. *This is instead of that.* He was God's Passover Lamb with a sign over his head declaring whom he belonged to, just like the lambs wore signs around their necks. Reuben couldn't hear what they were talking about but he was startled when Ethan called out to Peter.

"What shall we do then?"

"Repent and be baptized, every one of you, in the name of Jesus Christ so that your sins may be forgiven."

Ethan's arm wrapped around his wife and they moved forward. Reuben stepped towards them just as Judith turned and saw him. Ethan drew Reuben between them and Reuben had never seen such a look of love as when Judith gazed at him.

"Do you know what the name Reuben means?" Judith asked, looking from Ethan to Reuben. "It means, *Behold, a son.*"

Reuben stood in silence, not quite knowing what Judith meant by that statement.

"What we're saying is we'd like you to come home with us and be our son. My Kaddish."

Reuben slowly nodded his head, not quite believing what he had heard. *They ask much of me. I will be their son and in exchange they will be assured of someone to recite Kaddish, the mourner's prayer for eleven months after their death and then every year.*

"My parents are old and grieving over the fact we have no children," Ethan continued. "Would you like to be part of our family?"

"I am honoured." Reuben finally replied. "My father always said, 'If we recite Kaddish, praise to God, at the end of our Torah reading, should we not do the same at the end of a person's life?'"

"I'm a shepherd, in Bethlehem," Ethan stated. "We raise sheep and shear them and Judith spins the wool and weaves the robes and blankets we sell. You would be a great help to us and I know my father would love to take you into the hills with him and teach you how to use a sling."

"But first we must follow Peter's instructions and be baptized," Judith suggested.

The crowd had grown into the thousands, but as Peter and the other disciples answered questions about baptism local people stepped forward offering the use of the *miqveh* in their homes. The original followers of Jesus soon had people sorted out and directed towards the dozens of these facilities where fresh water was channeled into the hewn stone chambers in their homes. By the end of the day 3000 people had been baptized including Reuben and his new parents, Judith and Ethan.

"I don't know what we should do now," Ethan said quietly. "We need to learn more about The Way before we return to Bethlehem."

"We could stay here in the city for a few days," Reuben suggested. "Those who believe in Messiah Jesus meet every day at Solomon's Porch. The priests deny us access to the Temple but they can't deny us access to the outer courts."

Judith and Ethan exchanged a glance. Reuben could tell by their eyes that the idea pleased them.

Reuben couldn't miss the approval shining from Tirus' eyes when they arrived back at the inn and he heard that Ethan and Judith had finally dealt with their past grief and would take Reuben home with them as their own son. He wrapped Reuben in a huge hug.

I am getting lots of hugs these days. Not like when I was a leper and no one touched me for more than four years. Reuben squeezed the man tight, this man who had guided him to the temple for his cleansing.

The following two days Reuben led Ethan and Judith to the place where his friends met every day and like thirsty plants they absorbed everything people shared about what Jesus had taught them.

"Before he died, Jesus told us to remember him when we break bread together," one of the disciples reminded them as they gathered in Solomon's Porch.

Andrew's family invited them to their home to take part in this new teaching. There was a large group of believers that gathered and it seemed each one had something to say about the great blessings they had received that week.

They sang songs of praise to their creator and thanked him for sending His son as the ultimate Passover Lamb, to die for them. Then Andrew's father stood up.

"Jesus gave us these instructions before he died," he stated. "He ate with his disciples and then he broke a loaf of bread, explaining that it was to be a symbol that his body would be broken for us. Then he took a cup of wine and told them it was to be a symbol of his blood, shed for our sins."

Each of the believers shared in the bread and the wine and then Andrew's father continued to teach them.

"This is what Jesus told us to do, so we do this. While others still sacrifice a lamb at the temple and eat it together at home, we partake of the bread and the wine, symbols of his body and his blood as Jesus our Passover Lamb instructed us to do."

✡ ✡ ✡

"I STUDIED AT *BET HASEFER* until I got leprosy.' Reuben stated as his new parents escorted him along the road to Bethlehem. "But I haven't learned anything since then. Will I be able to go learn more in Bethlehem? I am sixteen now in size, but I am only twelve in learning."

"You are an adult now; you can go to the synagogue and study with the Levites. You will learn quickly, I'm sure," Judith replied.

"Why were you so sad in Jerusalem?" Reuben finally worked up the nerve to ask a question that had been bothering him. "Why were you crying while everyone else was celebrating when Jesus rode into the city?"

Then Ethan and Judith told him about their baby, Jair. How he died to provide a safe journey for the Messiah to Egypt when Herod was killing all the baby boys in Bethlehem. Reuben finally understood as Judith told him about seeing Jesus coming into the city and the people cheering for the King of the Jews.

"We blamed him for our son's death," she explained, "and we were devastated. We watched the crucifixion with anger in our hearts."

"I saw you there," Reuben replied.

"You were there?" Ethan gazed in shock at Reuben. "You were there alone?"

Reuben didn't reply and was silent for several minutes.

"I saw him!" Reuben suddenly blurted out.

"Saw who?" Judith and Ethan both asked at once.

"I saw Jesus, alive, after he was crucified."

Chapter 10

ETHAN AND JUDITH LISTENED in amazement as Reuben told them of his trip to Galilee with Andrew and Yakira. The couple hardly seemed to breathe as their chosen son reinforced their newfound belief in the Messiah.

Reuben told them about his delight in the temple and how much he had learned in the weeks since they had last seen him.

"I had never been in the temple until I went to be declared clean. It is so big. Some days I just walked around and looked at things and listened to people talk. I don't know how they could pile such huge stones on top of each other."

"I was about your age when Herod started building this temple," Ethan stated. "When Moses led our people out of Egypt, God gave them the plans for the tabernacle where He could dwell among his people. Our ancestors carried that tabernacle around with them until Solomon built a temple not quite as large as this one. It was destroyed a long time ago when our people were taken into exile to Babylon.

"Some of our people chose not to return from their places of exile but they come to celebrate the High Feasts with us. That's why there are so many languages spoken by our people, Judith stated."

"That's right," Ethan continued. "When God brought our people back home to Jerusalem Zarrubbabel repaired the temple. Our people were ruled by five different rulers before the Maccabees came along and won our land back again. Our temple was repaired again later by the Maccabees."

"I know about the Maccabees." Reuben could hardly contain his excitement at all this new information. "We celebrated Hanukkah when I was young and at home with my family. It was a great miracle, yes?"

"It was indeed a great miracle," Judith added, "when there was only enough sacred oil for the temple menorah for one day."

"But that little bit of oil lasted for eight days!" Reuben was proud to be able to fill in the details. There seemed to be so little that he did remember of their history. "Then Judah Maccabee and his mighty army rode into Jerusalem and delivered the city from the Syrians."

"You have a good memory, Reuben." Ethan patted him on the shoulder. "It was four hundred years after that when Herod decided to work on the temple. By that time it was in poor shape but Herod was determined it would be larger and more beautiful than Solomon's temple, not for

God's glory, but for his own glory. Some areas outside the original walls he filled in with rubble to extend the Temple Mount."

"How did they build such high walls? I paced off the stones and they are fifteen steps long and four steps wide piled one on top of the other. How did they do that?" Reuben's puzzled eyes focused on Ethan.

"Herod was determined to do everything according to God's command and one of those commands was that there would be no sound of iron tools during the building of His house. So the huge stones were cut to size in the quarry north of the city. It took eight years for them to prepare all the stones and then three years to build the walls and the Temple Mount. Earthen ramps were built and the blocks were slid up them and into place on rollers, the ramps being raised higher and higher as the wall was built. The top of the wall is large enough for a team of oxen to walk side by side, and sometimes it took many yoke of oxen pulling together to slide an especially large stone to the top."

✡ ✡ ✡

REUBEN CHATTERED AWAY, telling of his forays into the temple, finding the northern gate left open at night for wayfarers, hearing the echo of gates being opened in the morning when he slept inside the Temple Mount.

"I went with other followers of The Way to the temple to pray every day and listened to them talk about the things Jesus taught when he met with them in Solomon's Porch."

By the time they arrived in Bethlehem a bond had been formed between them, with Jesus as the pivot point.

Reuben was disappointed that it was too late to meet Ethan's parents when they arrived in Bethlehem but he was excited as he entered his new home and realized this was where he would live from now on. Judith proudly showed him her loom, set up in the second room and Reuben picked up several rolegs and felt their softness.

"I will spin those into yarn like this," Judith showed him some of the spun wool. Some day you can watch me weave and I will make another robe for you."

"And I will teach you to be a shepherd and shear the sheep so Judith has more wool to spin," Ethan added. "My father will teach you how to use a sling."

"What will your mother teach me? She will be my grandmother. May I call her *Savtah?"*

"We will see what she will teach you. Maybe you will teach her," Ethan said softly.

Ethan produced a pallet for Reuben to sleep on and Judith moved a few storage jars to make a place for him to sleep in a corner of the main room.

Reuben was thrilled when Ethan invited him to join him in reciting *broche,* the last prayer that was said at night and the first one in the morning. Curled up on his mat, it was a long time before Reuben fell asleep. Everything was new for him, a new body, a new family, a new home and a new village. *The God of Israel has answered my prayer.*

The next morning it wasn't birds that woke him, but the scent of barley loaves baking in the hearth. Quickly he rolled off his mat, folded it and propped it in the corner.

"Good morning, my Kaddish," Ethan said with a huge smile as he ran his hand over Reuben's head which was now covered with short dark curls. "Did you sleep well?"

"After spending years sleeping on the steps of the inn, this was a very comfortable bed. Can I meet my new grandparents today?"

"You will meet them soon, but first I must explain something to you. My father, Noam, believes in the Messiah, but doesn't speak about it. My mother will not be happy when she hears Jesus is the Messiah and he is alive. Even here in Bethlehem we have to be careful what we say."

Reuben listened closely as Ethan sang, "Blessed art thou, O, Lord, our God, King of the universe, who causes to come forth bread from the earth." *Some day I will sing motzi at this table.* Reuben could hardly wait to wiggle his way into the heart of this entire family. He ate his fill of barley loaves, cheese, olives and dates.

"When I was a leper and I was hungry, I missed the dates most of all."

"You won't ever be hungry again," Ethan stated. "If you are ever hungry you let your mama know or help yourself to whatever you want. This is your home now and everything in it belongs to you too." Ethan picked up a bag, slung it over his shoulder and motioned for Reuben to follow him out the door.

"That is my parents' home," Ethan remarked as Reuben followed him through the narrow streets of Bethlehem right to the edge of the village. "We won't go in just now. We'll go and meet my father first." They went around the house and took a path that wove back and forth, down a steep slope, leaving the village homes behind. Ahead of them lay hills, groves of olive trees, pastures up higher on the slopes. Rounding an outcrop of rock Reuben was surprised to see the sheepcote, an open rock cave in the side of the hill, almost right under the house above. An older man was bent over, examining a large ram, running his hands over its head, ears, up and down it's legs and under it's belly.

"Father, this is my new son, Reuben, my *Kaddish.* Reuben, this is my father, Noam, your new grandfather, your *Sabba.*" Reuben noticed how slowly the old man straightened up, as if his back needed olive oil to make the bones work.

"Reuben. Welcome to our family. My son has told me much about you. We will have many times with the sheep on the hills when you can tell me your story and I will tell you stories from the past." He loosed the ram and immediately another sheep came to him. "Come, put your hand on this ewe. Her name is Gentle Praise." Gently Noam guided Reuben's hands over the animal, all the time explaining to him how they were checking for cuts or scratches or sore spots.

"Does every animal have a name?" Reuben asked.

"Every one. You will learn to know their habits and soon know how they got their names. This young one," Noam pulled a younger sheep near to Reuben, "is named Curious. He was always wandering off and getting lost until one day he fell over a cliff and broke his leg. I had to carry him around for weeks and since then he never leaves my side."

The day flew past as they finished checking the animals and then led them up into the hills to a shady area. In spite of the summer heat, the grass was moist and green.

Reuben imitated the men as they found places to sit on the side of the hill where they could watch the sheep. He was surprised that when an animal seemed to be wandering away, Noam or Ethan would call its name and it would slowly turn and wander back. Noam told Reuben stories of how each sheep was named. When the sun was directly overhead, Ethan pulled open the bag he had carried and revealed an array of food that soon filled the empty spots inside.

"Come, you must learn to use a sling if you are going to protect the sheep," Noam stated.

"I have a sling that Ethan gave me but I have never learned how to use it."

"Then we will practice here on the hillside." Reuben listened attentively as Noam showed him how to choose the stones, how to whirl the sling about his head and send the rock flying at the right time. They all laughed together as Reuben's shots went wild, in every direction except the one where he wanted it to go.

"David must have spent many hours practicing before he slew Goliath," Reuben stated. "Did you know I saw King David's tomb in Jerusalem? My friend, Andrew took me to see it."

"David was a mighty soldier and a mighty man of God. You are becoming a mighty man of God too, Reuben."

The following day Reuben met Ayla, Ethan's mother. He was both nervous and excited as they entered the house. Ethan had explained that his cousin, Nina, was married and lived nearby but she often helped his mother. Ethan also warned him that his mother scorned any mention of Jesus.

"This is Reuben, our new son," Ethan stated as his mother turned from the hearth.

"Your wife cannot bear you a son so you find one on the streets of Jerusalem? So! He can live at your house. He is not welcome here." She turned away and spat on the floor. Ethan put his arm around Reuben's shoulder and turned him towards the door.

Chapter 11

"GO THEN! Leave your aging mother now you have found someone to take my place, yes?"

"No, mother, Reuben will not take your place. But he is my son and nothing you say will change that. Father is getting too old to climb date palms and so am I. It will be good to have a strong young man in the family. He is my Kaddish. I need someone to give God praise for my life some day too."

"I'M SORRY, REUBEN. My mother is a bitter woman. Some day I will tell you why. But we must have faith that she will come to understand that Jesus is our Messiah."

"She is not so bad. When I was a leper people called me names, yelled at me, threw stones at me, even spit on me. Your mother did none of those things. I like her. She will make a nice grandmother, my *savtah.* Maybe if I bring something sweet into her world, the bitterness will go away."

"Reuben, you are a wise young man. I am proud to have you for a son."

DAY AFTER DAY, while Ethan checked on their fruit trees and crops, Reuben went with Noam up into the hills to where the sheep could graze. Noam taught Reuben about David's shepherd psalm as he explained the art of raising sheep, showed him how to find green pastures and safe water. He explained how to dam up part of the channel, if the water was moving to swiftly, so even the lambs could drink. It reminded Rueben of the times Jesus referred to himself as a good shepherd. Within days Reuben was able to check the sheep for wounds or injuries and before long he took over the task of anointing cuts and scrapes with oil.

He loved the swooshing sound the sling made as he twirled it round and round above his head when he practiced. Sometimes the stone even went in the direction he wanted it to go.

When the Sabbath arrived Reuben was happy to once again be going to synagogue with a family. He was now a Son of the Covenant, but Judith and Ethan warned him again not to say everything that came to his mind. Reuben understood. He did not want to be banished from this synagogue.

TODAY A PORTION OF THE READING of the Torah was from the prophet Micah. Reuben understood many of the things the Messiah had been trying to teach them and hearing this portion of the Torah opened his eyes to even deeper understanding.

"What can we bring to the Lord?" The prophet Micah had written. *"What kind of offerings should we give him? Should we bow before God with offerings of yearling calves? Should we offer him thousands of rams and ten thousand rivers of olive oil? Should we sacrifice our first-born children to pay for our sin?*

No, O people, the Lord has told you what is good and this is what he requires of you. To do what is right, to love mercy and to walk humbly with your God."

After the reading of Torah, the offering of praise went heavenward in the form of Kaddish. They praised God for His great creation and blessed his name.

"*Blessed art thou, Lord our God, King of the universe, who has sanctified us with His commandments and commanded us to engross ourselves with the words of Torah.*

Please Lord, our God sweeten the words of your Torah in our mouths and in the mouths of all your people Israel."

Reuben was pleased that his memory had been refreshed and he could now recite most of the Kaddish along with everyone else, finishing with, *"May the Lord bless you and keep watch over you; May the Lord make His Presence enlighten you, and may He be kind to you; May the Lord bestow favor on you, and grant you peace."*

"Those are the things Jesus was teaching," Reuben said quietly to Ethan and Judith as they walked home later. "He told everyone to do what is right and be merciful and humble. I am so glad I can go to synagogue with you, here in Bethlehem."

✡ ✡ ✡

"I TALKED TO THE RABBI and you can begin lessons with him one day a week. You will soon remember all the things you learned at *bet hasefer* when you were younger. But be careful what you say to the Rabbi about your healing and about the Messiah."

"I will be careful," Reuben replied seriously. Busy weeks passed with Reuben learning something new every day, either in the hills with Noam, at *bet hasafer,* or helping Ethan and in every place his newfound faith in Messiah grew.

✡ ✡ ✡

"REUBEN, TODAY WE WILL BE harvesting the first figs," Ethan said as he put honey on his barley bread at breakfast time. "Have you ever climbed trees? Could you climb our fig trees and pick the figs for us?"

"I climbed trees with my brothers when I was little. Maybe I will still know how."

"My father will lead the sheep to pasture while the rest of us harvest figs."

"And I will get to know my *savtah.*" Reuben stuffed the rest of his food in his mouth so he would be ready to go. The older woman arrived at the door just then, carrying several large linen bags.

"I am going to climb the trees for you, *Savtah.*" There was excitement in Reuben's voice as he rushed to take the bags from her arms.

"Leave the bags! I am not so old that I cannot carry my own bags. I hope you have good feet for clinging onto the tree trunk and quick fingers for picking the fruit."

"I do now. When I was a leper I had no fingers and no toes. But since Jesus healed me I can do anything with my fingers. You'll see." Reuben walked out the door, not even noticing the astonished look on Ayla's face. Or the anger that flashed from her eyes a moment later.

The family had four fig trees and four date trees, just enough to provide them with fruit for each year. Judith tucked a bag into Reuben's belt as Ethan explained what he had to do.

"And don't bring down any mushy figs," Ayla snarled. "They will sour. And don't pick any green ones because the juice from the stem will burn your hands."

It took Reuben a couple attempts before he finally discovered the way to climb the tree, leaning away from the tree with a hand and foot on each side of the trunk as he walked his way up. He was careful to pick only the fruit his *savtah* told him, leaving any that were still a bit green or mushy. His sack was full when he slowly made his way down to the ground again.

"There are three trees left to do and you are so slow. I could go up that tree faster than you." Ayla grabbed the full bag and handed him another one. Reuben grinned at her.

"We could have a race and see who wins. The young strong one, or the old wise one."

"Get up that tree," Ayla barked, but Reuben saw a little twitch of a smile at the corners of her mouth. Reuben had asked Ethan how old his parents were and knew Ayla had passed eighty years. He was also aware that Ethan and Judith were both past fifty when they took him as their son.

It took all day to pick the figs. Ethan carried two bags home on his back while Judith and Ayla each balanced a bag on their head. Reuben tried to carry one that way, but it fell on the ground and Ayla scolded him.

"All the figs will be bruised. For shame!" Reuben grinned at her again and picked up the bag. "That was not so much work," the elderly woman continued. "In the spring my son moves the pollen from the male trees to the female trees. Up and down, up and down he goes all day. You only went up and down four times. Not so much!"

"Next spring can I help you do that, yes?" Reuben looked at Ethan with hope in his eyes.

"You can help, yes. Maybe help with one and do all the rest yourself, yes?"

Over the next five days Judith and Ayla took care of drying the figs in the sun and Reuben went back to helping with the sheep.

"I like my new *savtah,"* Reuben told Noam as they sat on the hillside the next day. "I almost made her smile once. Some day I will make her smile."

"So you learned how to harvest the figs, yes?"

"I did. And it was fun climbing the trees."

"Yes, it is fun climbing the fig trees, but in a couple weeks it will be time for the date harvest. Climbing a date palm is not so much fun."

"But I like dates. No matter how hard, it will be worth it."

Day after day as the summer heat increased they sought shade both for the sheep and for themselves. Sometimes in the evening Reuben drew water from the well for the sheep because the day had been so hot.

✡ ✡ ✡

HIS WEEKLY STUDY at the synagogue was like water to his own dry, thirsty soul as little by little he remembered things from the Torah that he had learned as a child. Then date harvest was upon them and Reuben discovered Noam was right. Climbing a date palm was hard work. The trunk of the tree was covered with sharp bumps where palm fronds had grown and died off.

"While the tree was growing I cut the thorns off," Ethan explained. "The thorns are long and sharp enough to cut right through your flesh."

"Here, Reuben. I have special sandals for you to wear today for climbing these trees." Judith handed him a pair of sandals of woven papyrus that would protect his feet from the rough bark. Then she tied several bags around his waist.

"Put the bag around the dates before you cut the frond, then shake the dates off into the bag and throw the frond to the ground. When a bag is full I will come up and get it," Ethan stated.

"You climb the tree now," his mother scolded. "This boy cannot do a man's job."

"This boy, my son, wants to do a man's job. Don't you Kaddish?"

Reuben nodded, excitement beaming from his brown eyes. It took him several tries before he got his balance and began to climb steadily up the tree, the bumps actually providing narrow footholds as he climbed.

Then his foot slipped and suddenly he was sliding back down the tree, the protrusions scraping his legs as his hands frantically fought for a grip. Finally, he caught hold of the tree and clung tightly until his feet found traction again. Once at the top, the burning scratches were quickly forgotten in his amazement at the huge heavy clusters of dates hanging from the thick fronds.

They worked all day, but Reuben was so enthralled in learning everything he could about dates that he didn't even notice the time go by. Every bag full of dates that Ethan retrieved from the top of the tree made Reuben's heart swell.

"*Savtah*! When we eat dates in the winter I will remember that I helped to pick them," he hollered down to where Judith and Ayla were sorting the dates as he came down the tree.

"If any of them last that long," Ayla muttered loudly. "He is so rough maybe they will all be rotten by then."

"Then I will mash them up and spread them on my barley loaf. They would still taste better than some of the things I ate when I was a leper." Ayla, with a thoughtful look on her face, stared after Reuben as he walked away.

THEY HAD HARDLY FINISHED getting the dates sorted and stored for the winter when it was time to harvest the summer figs and everything started over again. Reuben was thankful for his lightweight linen garments that moved with every little breeze. He sighed in weary relief when he lay down at night but as he thought back over what he had done that day he felt proud that he could be so useful. *Ethan and Judith really did need a son and Sabba needed a grandson. Savtah needed a grandson too but she doesn't know it yet.*

WE'RE GOING BACK TO JERUSALEM! Reuben had watched the pile of robes and blankets grow higher every week. He knew that sooner or later, Judith and Ethan would take them to Jerusalem to sell. But would they allow him to go along?

"We are going back to Jerusalem!" It was the first thing he told Noam when he saw him in the morning. "The date and fig harvests are all finished and we will be in Jerusalem for Rosh Hashanah"

"That will be a good break for all of you," Noam replied. "You will be able to see your friends and be back home before the first rains. After that we will be busy ploughing and planting before the main rains come."

"There is sure a lot of work to do when you are a shepherd and a farmer."

"We are thankful to have such a strong son and grandson. You will learn how to do all these things and some day, all this will belong to you. When the ploughing is done it will be time for olive harvest."

"We will be back here for Sukkot, the Festival of Booths. Last year I stayed with my friend Andrew and his family in their booth. But it is not the same as having your own."

"You will be excited to see The Temple again, too?"

"*Sabba*, did you know the the beautiful curtain hanging at our Most Holy Place was torn from the top to the bottom? There was an earthquake at the time of the evening sacrifice and the huge gates opened all by themselves and lintal broke and fell. I saw the big mess and everyone was running around. The priests had not even had time to wash away all the blood."

"Yes, I heard about that and that the Sanhedrin had to move out of their beautiful Chamber of Hewn Stones and meet in the Trading Place. It would seem that their decision to put our Messiah to death was the last decision they made inside The Temple walls."

"It seems like every time the Lord is displeased with our people he allows the temple to be destroyed and everyone taken into exile. Do you think that will happen again? He must be very displeased, like that story Jesus told of the man who owned a vineyard and left men in charge of it. They killed every servant who came to collect his money and finally killed his son too."

"Yes, sometimes I fear what will happen to us because Messiah was put to death."

"So many strange things have happened this past year. Messiah came and healed me and gave me back my life and then he healed Judith. I watched as they put him to death but Jesus came back to life and I saw him alive again. I wish I could have seen him go up to heaven in a cloud but he sent the gift of his Spirit, like he promised."

"It was indeed a strange year. It was also the year that brought you to us."

"I can hardly wait to see Tirus again and tell him about all the things I have learned. He will laugh when I tell him about climbing the trees to pick figs and dates and everything I have learned about looking after the sheep."

That night, as he lay in his bed, Reuben thought about his introduction to lambing season. It was a time of both birth and death. A young ewe died giving birth to her first offspring. Reuben loved the little orphan lamb but he quickly learned that he couldn't let his heart stand in the way of the work. Another lamb had died and Noam showed Reuben how to skin the dead lamb and tie it's hide over that little orphan lamb. It was the only way the ewe would accept the orphan and nurse it in place of her own. *I didn't like dragging that one tiny lamb on the ground either.*

Noam had given Reuben the job of moving a ewe and her lamb closer to the flock because she had wandered away and given birth where they couldn't see her. Grabbing the lamb by the back legs, Reuben had to drag it along the ground so the ewe would follow the scent of the lamb. The tiny, terrified, bleats as the tiny lamb was dragged along almost broke his heart.

It was a while before he could sleep, just thinking of the day. Especially the tiny lambs that had been designated for temple sacrifice. Some day Ethan would take them to Jerusalem. Given to the LORD to die. It's too hard for me to think about when I'm tired.

Chapter 12

REUBEN HELPED ETHAN tie the load of robes and blankets onto the donkey. Even though the road to Jerusalem was dry and dusty after the heat of summer the trip was an exciting one for Reuben. He talked most of the way.

"*Sabba* has even given me two lambs of my own, did you know that?"

"I didn't know that," Judith replied, "but it is something Noam would do. He loves you." As they neared the city they tried to keep away from all the dust that puffed up behind the camel trains from Egypt.

Tirus grinned from ear to ear as he welcomed them again to his inn. Reuben had grown even taller and stronger in the four months he had been gone. He seemed to be everywhere at once helping to set up the booth and arrange their goods. His help made the work faster and as he worked Reuben told Tirus about his new way of life.

"Maybe you want to go and find Andrew," Ethan said when everything was in place. Reuben hurried off and spent hours retelling the story of his new life to Andrew.

"Do you still meet on the Temple Mount every day? My parents and I will meet your family there tomorrow." Reuben felt a strange thrill go through him as he referred to Ethan and Judith as his parents. "Did you know I have a new *sabba*? He has taught me how to use a sling."

On the first Sabbath of the ten-day celebration Reuben and his new parents went to the synagogue before going to the temple. The Torah reading for the day was Moses' instructions to the Levites for the Day of Atonement and as they listened Reuben had a picture in his mind of the priest who had performed the cleansing ceremony for him.

Andrew and his family invited them to their home.

"Others of The Way will be there too," Andrew's father told them. "It seems like every day we have new people joining us. As people hear more about Jesus they realize he really is Messiah and they want to follow him. We meet at the temple to worship and we are continually learning. We are beginning to see Messiah in every part of The Torah, in things we have read before but never understood."

They paused to allow a distinguished looking group of young men walk past following a teacher.

"That is the great teacher Gamaliel and some of his students, brilliant men who will one day be part of the Sanhedrin. Each one is studying to be a minister, teacher and lawyer, taking all the classes at once. Those men will become respected Pharisees, the most highly educated authorities of the Law." They watched the esteemed group walk down the street.

"We fellowship and break bread at our homes," Andrew's father continued to explain to them the pattern the believers had adopted"

"Can we go to the temple for Yom Kippur?" Reuben asked. It took place on the tenth day of the festival, a day of fasting, the Day of Atonement. "I know Messiah was the Lamb of God, offered once for all but I've never seen what happens on this great day when the High Priest goes into the Most Holy Place. Just to see? Please?"

"Come with us first to synagogue, and then you can still go to the temple to watch the final sacrifice of the bull and the goat and see the scapegoat released into the wilderness."

"We could do that, yes?" Ethan turned to question Reuben, whose face shone with excitement.

"Yes! We could do that."

✡ ✡ ✡

THEY HAD A BUSY WEEK and Reuben could hardly contain himself, waiting for the Day of Atonement when he would watch this celebration for the first time. When the day finally arrived the two families walked through the throngs of people to the overflowing synagogue. After the Torah was taken from its cupboard and paraded around the room, it was laid on the podium. Today, seven portions would be read and seven people called up to recite the blessing, *alijah,* for each portion.

This day the story of Jonah was read and that brought to Reuben's mind what people had learned from Jesus' teaching. Jonah's three days and three nights in the belly of the whale was a sign to the people that Jonah was sent by God. *Jesus said that what would happen to the Son of Man would also be a sign to the people that he was sent by God.* Reuben quickly made the connection between Jonah's experience and Jesus being three days and three nights in the tomb.

Reuben's eyes darted back and forth as they entered the temple, attempting to see everything at one. With more than five hundred priests assisting the high priest, the place was even more crowded than usual.

He couldn't miss the high priest adorned in a blue robe, woven without a seam, trimmed with blue, purple and scarlet pomegranates and golden bells around the hem. His breastplate contained the colours of the sanctuary, white, blue, purple and scarlet but was also decorated with twelve precious stones to represent the twelve tribes of Israel. These four extra pieces of clothing he wore today, as well as the four linen items the ordinary priests wore.

Reuben nudged Ethan and ran his hand across his forehead, nodding towards the high priest. Ethan nodded back. The *Ziz*, a golden plate, stretched across the front of the high priest's turban, a symbol of royalty and engraved on it was 'Holiness unto Jehovah'.

By the time they arrived at the temple the morning sacrifices were finished. A ram had been sacrificed for the priests, a young bullock, a ram, seven lambs and one kid for the congregation, plus their meat and drink offerings.

Arrayed in his splendid garments, the high priest was about to enter into their Most Holy Place.

Then the man disappeared from Reuben's sight for a time. When he appeared again Reuben was amazed to discover he had taken off all his finery, bathed and put on ordinary white linen garments, the same as all the other priests were wearing.

"The high priest has been practicing all week so he will not make a mistake as he sprinkles blood, burns incense, lights the lamp and offers the daily sacrifice," Ethan whispered to Reuben. "He will also bathe and change his clothing five times and wash his hands and feet ten times during this day."

Reuben pushed through the crowd until he was right against the railing that divided the Court of the Israelites from the Court of the Priests. Now he could see two identical goats, both part of the same offering, facing towards the temple. Ethan had explained to him what would take place during this most important feast, but Reuben wanted to see for himself.

A young bull stood between the altar and the Temple and the high priest laid both his hands on the animal's head and confessed his sin.

"Ah, LORD, I have committed iniquity; I have transgressed; I have sinned—I and my house. I entreat thee to cover over our iniquities, transgressions and sins which I have committed against thee, I and my house as it is written in the Law of Moses." Three times he mentioned the name of the Lord and each time the people closest to him bowed down with their faces on the ground and all the congregation cried, "Blessed be the Name; the glory of His kingdom is for ever and ever."

Off to the side a golden urn had caught Reuben's eye. He had never seen anything so beautiful and wondered what it was for. He didn't have long to wait, for just then the high priest walked over, picked up the urn and shook it. Then putting both hands inside he withdrew two objects of the same size, shape and weight and set them on the heads of the goats.

"They are the lots, drawn to see which goat is the scapegoat," Ethan whispered. "One is labeled 'for Jehovah' and the other says 'for Azazel' (separated). That one will be sent into the wilderness."

The high priest tied a tongue-shaped piece of red cloth to the horn of the one whose lot said 'for Azazel' and turned that goat to face the people He tied an identical red cloth around the neck of the goat that would be offered as a sacrifice and left it facing the altar. *I wonder which one is the most important. It must be the one to be sacrificed.*

Placing his hands again on the young bull, the high priest prayed the same prayer again, but this time he confessed the sins of the priesthood. Immediately, he killed the young bull as a sin offering for himself, his family and the priests. Catching the blood in a bowl, he handed it to another priest whose job it was to keep the bowl constantly moving to prevent the blood from coagulating until the high priest was ready for it.

Picking up a brass fire pan of burning coals and a dish full of incense the high priest approached the gleaming white limestone Temple. He ascended a short flight of stair, entered the porch and proceeded through the Holy Place where every day priests took turns trimming the wicks on the seven-branched candlestick, offering incense, and looking after the table that held the bread.

What followed was the high priest's most important ministry of the entire year, his journey into the sacred Holy of Holies. Reuben held his breath as he disappeared behind the heavy dividing curtain where he was only allowed to go once a year. Today was that day.

"The Most Holy Place is dark except for the glow from the burning coals he carries," Ethan whispered. "No one but the high priest can even look into that place. He will set the coals down on the foundation stone, where the ark once sat and scatter the incense upon the hot coals filling the room with smoke."

When Reuben was attending bet hasefer as a young boy he had learned about that smoke-filled Holy of Holies, but at that time it was The Shikinah Glory, the presence of the Lord that filled the tabernacle with smoke.

I would love to see God's presence fill this place with smoke. That must have been a wonderful sight and scary too.

Reuben was sad to think that there was nothing behind that curtain except the foundation stone. Their beloved Ark of the Covenant had disappeared during a raid on the temple decades earlier. *Is it still a Most Holy Place even without the Ark?*

Suddenly a sigh of relief went through the crowd as the high priest came backing out from behind the curtain, praying as he did so that they would not be taken captive in the following year. He took the blood, that the other priest had kept constantly moving, and went in a second time to sprinkle the blood towards the place where the mercy seat had once covered over the Ark.

"He will sprinkle the blood up and down seven times, counting each motion so he does not make a mistake."

While the people anxiously waited for him to come back out, Reuben, along with everyone else, remembered stories about strange things that happened in that holy place.

Zacharias, the high priest, was struck dumb in the Holy of Holies when an angel gave him the promise of a son, and he didn't believe that message from God. He couldn't talk until after his son was born. If an angel ever talked to me I would believe him.

When the high priest finally backed out again from the Most Holy Place and set the bowl of blood outside the curtain everyone breathed another sigh of relief.

Next he killed the sacrificial goat and entered a third time into the Most Holy Place, this time with the goat's blood.

Reuben pictured in his mind what he had been told the high priest would be doing in that place this time. How he would sprinkle the goat's blood in the same manner and then sprinkle the blood of both animals towards the curtain inside. Once again the high priest came backing out and now he sprinkled the blood of both animals towards the curtain outside the Holy of Holies. Finally, he mixed the blood of the two and sprinkled the horns of the altar of incense, and what was left of the blood he poured out on the west side of the altar of burnt offering. Every part of the temple, the Most Holy Place, the veil, the Holy Place, the altar of incense and the altar of burnt offering had now been anointed and were cleansed from the defilement of the priesthood and the worshippers.

Laying his hands on the head of the scapegoat, the high priest prayed another prayer of repentance. Then he led the animal out through Solomon's Porch and through the eastern gate to be sent off into the wilderness. Reuben remembered his own cleansing from leprosy, when one bird had been killed and the other let go free.

"How can someone take the scapegoat all the way to the wilderness and not break the law about walking more than a Sabbath Day's journey?" Reuben whispered to Ethan.

"Ten men went out last night before sundown and stationed themselves all along the route. The goat will be passed from one person to another, each one leading it another Sabbath's Day's journey. The tenth person will lead it to the edge of the wilderness, tear off part of the red cloth and fasten it to a rock and the scapegoat will be pushed over the crest of a rock into the wilderness. Then with the waving of flags the signal will be sent back the same route all the way to the temple indicating that the goat has borne all our iniquities into a land not inhabited."

"What happens to that piece of red cloth?"

"During the year, that red cloth will turn from red to white indicating that, as Isaiah has written, though their sins were red like crimson they would be white as snow."

While the scapegoat was being taken to the wilderness, Reuben watched the high priest cut up the bull and the other goat and send the carcasses to be burnt outside the city at the Place of the Ashes. Finally, he went into the Court of Prayer, read the law the Lord had given Moses concerning the Levites and prayed.

There was still work to be done. There were festive burnt offerings to be made and the animals, whose blood had been sprinkled in the Most Holy Place, had yet to be placed on the altar before the final evening sacrifice took place.

Reuben noticed the high priest had removed his white linen garments and put on the gold-trimmed raiment again before he carried out all those offerings. Then for the final time, he donned the white linen robes and went a fourth time into that Holy of Holies to fetch the censer and incense dish which he had left there.

"When he takes off his linen garments they will never be used again. Priest's robes are never washed or worn again," Ethan whispered. "They are made into wicks for the temple lamps."

The high priest washed his hands and feet, burned the evening incense and lit the lamps on the candlestick for the night. Then he washed again and put on his own clothes to be escorted by the people to his home in Jerusalem. The fasting was over and the feast began.

As they left the city Reuben was sad to say good-bye again to Andrew, but he was looking forward to putting up a shelter of their own for the Feast of Tabernacles. It came to Reuben's mind that he had now lived for seventeen years.

THIS YEAR AT THE FEAST OF TABERNACLES Reuben was elated that not only would he be part of a family again, but have a *Sabba* and *Savtah* too. He eagerly assisted them in setting up their booth on the open roof of their house. Ayla bossed him around, making him do everything twice so it was done to her liking.

"Everything is good if it is done twice, yes?" Reuben grinned at Ayla. Then he deliberately hung the red pomegranates at odd angles so his *savtah* would scold him and make him re-hang them to her satisfaction.

"I am glad that I have fingers again so I can help you decorate the booth," Reuben stated. "Before Jesus healed me, I only had half of my fingers and toes."

"Don't mention that man!" Ayla spat on the floor. "He was an imposter."

"But I saw him die on the cross," Reuben told her. "And then after that I saw him alive in Galilee. I walked all the way to Galilee to see him and there he was. He must have been special to God for him to do such a thing."

"Go into the house and help your mother!" Ayla banished him from the rooftop, but not before Reuben saw the speculation in her eyes. *She called Judith my mother.* Reuben jumped down the stairs in three big leaps.

Chapter 13

"TODAY WE MUST PLOUGH THE FIELDS," Ethan stated one morning as they were eating breakfast. "My father will take the sheep to pasture and you can help me with the ploughing. Maybe by the end of the day you will be doing it yourself."

Reuben was eager to get started on this new learning process. He watched closely as Ethan put the harness on the donkey, explaining every step and how important it was to have everything fitting properly so the harness didn't rub on the animal and cause sores. Then he hooked up the plough and the work began.

Ethan told Reuben how to set his sights on something in the distance so his furrows would be straight. By the time he finished his first turn at the plow Reuben's muscles were aching. It was hard work keeping pressure on the wooden handles so the plowshare made a deep furrow. He rested while Ethan ploughed and then was ready to try it again.

This is really hard work, trying to prevent the plough from jumping around and keep it moving in a straight line as well as keeping the donkey going.

As he went to bed that night he was proud of the work he had done, but didn't look forward to day after day of such hard work. After the ploughing was finished it would be time to harvest the olives. *I didn't realize how much they needed a son when I asked them that day in Jerusalem. I am glad I can help them but I would like to help my savtah too.*

Olive harvest wasn't nearly as hard as the fig and date harvests had been and almost seemed like a holiday after ploughing. Robes were laid beneath the tree and the olives were so ripe they just fell off when the tree was hit with long sticks. Judith insisted the rest was a woman's job although she did let Reuben take a turn at the olive press in case she ever needed help.

"Before Jesus healed me I was in so much pain that Ethan had to press the olives for me. Now I am so thankful to be free of pain that it is a job I do with joy."

Reuben put all his energy into rolling the upright, round stone over the olives that had been pitted and poured into a round trough. He was amazed at the amount of oil that poured out. Judith set aside the oil from the first pressing to be used for their lamps and ointments. Reuben pressed the pulp again and could hardly believe how much oil still flowed out. Over and over he rolled the heavy stone over the olive pulp until there was no more oil to extract. He was pleased that he could help his mother with this heavy job and amazed at how much he had learned. *I will never take an oil lamp for granted again.*

"Hanukkah is coming soon and I have been noticing that you have been growing again. Perhaps it's time I made you some new clothes."

Reuben looked down and his robe was short. Had he grown that much?

"All the wool is in baskets in the corner. Why don't you pick out the colours you'd like for the stripes? Once the rains start I'll have more time for weaving."

Reuben didn't rush through this chore as he sorted through the spun wool, squeezing the soft bundles in his hands, rubbing it against his cheek. He finally chose a rusty brown and a dark brown and carried them to Judith.

Ethan was still learning how to be a father but Noam was like an answer to Reuben's dreams. Reuben couldn't remember his own grandparents, who died when he was quite young, but his new *sabba* told stories and every story had a lesson in it for Reuben to learn.

"I remember some of the stories about Hanukkah," Reuben said one day when that festival came up. "Did you ever meet any of the Maccabees?"

Noam laughed and slapped his leg.

"I'm old, but I'm not that old. That all happened four hundred years ago."

WITHIN WEEKS REUBEN was back at Ethan's side learning about planting flax, barley and wheat in their three fields.

They walked the ploughed fields, scattering the seeds because within a short time the main rains of the year would be upon them. As Ethan explained how to scatter the seeds, Reuben realized he had already learned about that when one of Jesus' disciples retold a story Jesus had told.

"Jesus told a story about sowing grain," Reuben told Ethan as they stopped for a rest. "Some of the grain fell on the hard path, some fell on stony ground, some among weeds and thistles and some in good soil like this area we ploughed."

"I can imagine what happened to the seed," Ethan replied. "Some didn't grow at all, some sprouted but didn't grow very well, and what was planted in good soil brought forth a good crop, yes?"

"That's right, but Jesus said the seed is his word and the places where the seed falls are different kinds of hearts. Some people have hard hearts, like our scriptures talk about Pharaoh, hardening his heart. Some people allow past experiences to keep the seed from growing and others let their worries and cares choke out the word."

"That leaves just the last type," Ethan said thoughtfully. "Like us, where the seed of his word has found good soil and is growing strong."

"I'm glad Jesus told stories. When I'm sowing the seed I can understand what he wanted us to learn and I will be careful to sow the seed where we've ploughed. When I help *Sabba* with the sheep, I understand what Jesus meant about being a shepherd too." *But we can plough up those hard packed places and pull out the thistles and thorns. Maybe that can happen with hearts too.*

"I'm glad we have good soil. The flax is our fastest growing crop so within three months, when it is in bloom, we will harvest it and Judith will begin to prepare it for making linen garments."

Reuben found he could be a great help as his mother began filling kettle after kettle with water to dye her wool. He was startled to realize onion skins turned the wool brown; red poppies made orange wool and certain berries turned it light blue. When Judith was satisfied with a colour the heavy water-soaked wool was lifted out of the water and hung up to dry. Reuben insisted on helping with that job.

"Wait!" Reuben paused with a load of heavy, wet wool half-way out of the water. "That wool has been dyed with turmeric and needs to be put into lye water to turn it red. Put it in here. I have already soaked ashes in this kettle to make lye water."

Reuben lowered the heavy wet wool into the water his mother had prepared and together they watched it change colour. Reuben caught sight of his father leaning against the door, a smile on his face as he watched his wife talk about her love of colours.

"Now, this is my most precious dye," Judith stated. "It is a secretion milked from the murex sea snail at Tyre. It is expensive but over the years my business has grown so now I can afford to buy it. It turns the wool purple, the symbol of royalty. But I don't weave that wool. I take it as an offering to the temple to be used there."

Looking at Judith's head bent over her expensive dye, Reuben was startled to see the white in her hair. Once again he was reminded that they were aging.

The rains began to fall outside but the family was warm and dry. Ethan was sharpening the plowshares, getting them ready for the next year. Reuben was oiling harness. As he worked Reuben watched his mother wind yarn between two stakes pounded into the floor at the precise distance apart according to the length she wanted the item being woven. When she lifted the yarn off the stakes with a rod and carried it to the loom Reuben wiped his hands and followed her, curious to see what she was doing.

"Ethan made this loom for me before our son, Jair, was born. And Jacob made these disks for me, the weights that hold each yarn tight. These are called the heddles," she explained, pointing out an amazing number of knotted cords hanging from two horizontal shafts. "I will thread a strand of yarn through the center loop on each of the heddles. Here, put your foot on this pedal." Reuben pushed on the pedal and one of the shafts lifted, taking every other heddle with it. "Now step on the other one." Reuben pushed on the opposite foot pedal and the other shaft lifted taking the opposite heddles with it. "You will see how it works once I get it all set up."

Reuben went back to his work, hearing the rain falling outside, the scraping of Ethan's file on the plowshare and Judith quietly preparing her loom for weaving. A peace settled in his heart. *The Lord has blessed me beyond measure.*

The following day Reuben went out to help Noam with the sheep that were huddled in the sheepcote to keep dry. Then Noam took Reuben home with him.

"I have brought our grandson home so you can feed him," Noam stated to his wife as they shook the raindrops off their outer garments.

"Yes! He looks like he is starving. Sit down and I will put some fat on your bones."

Reuben obediently sat down and Noam joined him while Ayla bustled about putting food in front of them. She added more and more dishes to the table and Noam looked at Reuben with a silly grin on his face.

"She likes to cook," he whispered.

"He's talking nonsense," Ayla replied, plunking a bowl down. "So eat already. What is happening at your house today? Nothing? They are napping that they can't feed you?"

"Judith is setting up the loom so she can weave and your son is sharpening the plowshares."

"Weaving! Weaving! That is all she does."

Reuben stared at her in confusion. *Why does she dislike my mother so much?*

"But I see you wear the garments she weaves," Noam said with a chuckle.

"Lest I get sick and die," Ayla shot back.

After eating until he was overfull Reuben stayed and listened to his *sabba* tell stories about the past.

✡ ✡ ✡

"I will never tire of seeing everything blooming and bearing fruit," Reuben stated one day as he walked beside their barley field with his father and grandfather. Fluffy almond trees dotted the landscape, frothy with pink blossoms.

"Do you harvest the almonds too?" Reuben asked his father.

"We only have two trees, but it's enough for us for the year. It's soon time to watch for the First Fruits. When we begin to see fruit on the figs, dates, almonds and olive trees we will go together to mark them and also the first fruits of our barley, wheat and flax. Those offerings will be our thanksgiving to the Lord for the rain and the sun and the earth."

"Will you go to Jerusalem with us, *Sabba*?" Reuben asked.

"No. Your *savtah* is not well enough to stay home alone so long and she can't walk that far. You will have to tell me all about your trip when you get back and all that you learn at the temple."

Reuben didn't know his *savtah* was sick, but later he realized that she didn't move as fast as she once did. A few days later Noam made a suggestion that shocked them all.

"Your mother has not been able to milk the goats for a while now so Judith has been doing it. I think it would be good if we trade houses. Our house has the extra room you built Ethan, when you and Judith got married. It would suit you. And your mother would not have so much to look after in your smaller house."

"It would be a big job to move the loom," Ethan replied, "but maybe some day."

Reuben began walking past the trees almost every day, watching for signs of fruit. A couple times he even climbed a tree to see if there wasn't something beginning to grow up there. He wanted to learn how to mark their first fruit offerings. When he saw the little rounds of fruit taking shape he reported it immediately. Then he waited to learn another lesson.

✡ ✡ ✡

"TOMORROW WE'LL BEGIN shearing the sheep," Ethan informed Reuben as they ate their evening meal after a day of hard work. "This year you can help. Maybe *Sabba* will teach you how to use the shears."

Early the next morning Ethan and Reuben met Noam at the sheepcote below his house. Judith went to spend the day with Ayla but planned to bring their noon lunch out to them.

"The sheep must be sheared in the spring or they will get too hot during the summer heat. We have already chosen the lambs that we will take to the temple as our first fruits of the flock." Reuben listened carefully as Noam explained which sheep they would be shearing and showed him the shears and how they worked.

"The wool contains a lot of lanolin oil, so it's important to keep cleaning the shears." Noam guided a large ram towards Ethan who stood waiting with the shears. He flipped the animal onto his back and began working the shears up the belly, the wool folding back as he sheared towards the side and down the legs.

"This part of the fleece is the most valuable," Ethan said as he cut up and over the back of the ram. "Judith will spin this wool directly from the fleece with the natural oils in it. Other portions of the wool will be carded and teased before she spins it."

Noam and Ethan took turns shearing while Reuben took his turn guiding the animals into place, rolling up the fleece when the last cut released it from the animals hide, and finally he took his turn with the shears.

"I'm afraid I will cut the ram," he stated as he hesitantly plied the shears along the animals hide. It took him a long time to train one hand to hold on to the sheep while the other hand manipulated the shears.

"You'll get used to it." Ethan stood nearby, ready to help if needed, but both men patiently waited, instructing Reuben which area to do next until he took the last cut and the fleece dropped to the ground.

"I did it!" Reuben stood up quickly, freeing the animal. "Ow! My back hurts." He reached around his waist to massage his lower back. Ethan and Noam both laughed. They knew exactly how painful it was to bend over an animal for so long, with the back of the sheep's head braced on your bent knees for part of that time. Reuben was glad to see Judith approaching with their noon meal and, bent over, he hobbled towards her to tell her what he had done. A grin creased his face as all three of them teased him about walking like an old man. It was easy also to spot the animal he had sheared by the uneven ridges left in tact.

Chapter 14

EVERYTHING HAD BEEN so new for Reuben the previous year that although he saw the family live out The Law, he didn't really grasp it all. He had never before seen crops grow, fruit harvested, sheep sheared or olives pressed and a portion of it given to the Lord. This year, everything made sense and he knew how to help.

Judith had been weaving blankets and robes and now she had new fleeces to work with. Usually considered a woman's job, Reuben sometimes helped her pull off the tags, the dirty parts of the fleece that she would use for coarse articles. He quickly learned to feel the bits of twigs and burrs buried in the wool and his nimble fingers would work until the unwanted speck was removed.

"I'm glad I have fingers so I can help you with this work." His parents exchanged a glance, smiling at how often they had heard him utter that statement.

Reuben eagerly awaited the flax harvest because that meant it would soon be time to return to Jerusalem for Passover. One day Reuben helped his mother and his *savtah* prepare troughs for retting the flax. Reuben had no idea what that meant but he soon discovered that flax harvest was like none he'd ever seen before. One hundred days after they planted the flax it was in bloom, blue flowers blowing in the wind like the waves on a lake.

"I've marked off this area to be left standing," Ethan told him. "That will be our seed for next year and those fibres will be tough. We'll use them to make string and rope."

Reuben helped his father pull the blooming plants out by the roots while Noam bundled them into sheaves, the blue flowers sticking out at each end.

Once the crop was harvested Reuben learned what the troughs were for.

"We need to soften the *bast*," Judith explained. "That's this tough outer stalk. So we'll leave the flax soaking in the troughs while we go to Jerusalem. By the time we get home that tough layer will be softened, almost rotten, giving us access to the linen fibres inside. Once we separate them I will spin them to make new linen garments for all of us."

✡ ✡ ✡

"HOW LONG DID IT TAKE THEM to build the temple?" Reuben asked Noam the day before their trip to Jerusalem. "I explored every part of the temple when I was all alone in Jerusalem but I don't understand it all. Have you been there lots of times?"

"I have been there many times for the festivals. Almost every other year we also took a newborn baby to be dedicated. But each time the baby would die. Until Ethan. He was the only one of our many babies that lived."

"I saw the place where the babies were dedicated. It was near the Leper's Chamber where I bathed and washed my clothes and shaved the second time."

"Will we celebrate Passover at the temple this year now that Messiah has come?" Reuben asked as they made their way towards the city. "Will we still take our lambs to the temple?" His parents looked at him in surprise.

"I don't know the answer to that question," his father stated. "We will have to ask the other believers when we see them."

"I would still like to go to the Temple," Reuben replied. "I've never seen the sacrifice of the Passover lambs."

The roads into Jerusalem were teeming with people headed to the city, many families bringing their Pascal lamb with them. By the time they arrived at the city gate they were being shoved and jostled by the crowd so they were thankful to arrive at the inn and begin putting up their booth and setting out their wares. That didn't take long with three of them working at it but people were stopping to buy robes and blankets before they were even ready for business.

The next morning Reuben woke to discover that his father had gone to visit Andrews's family. *I wonder why he went without me. Why did he go so early?*

When his father returned he explained.

"I went to talk to Andrew's father to learn more about the Messiah and if it has changed what we believe."

"What did he say? Will we still celebrate Passover like we always have?"

"Passover is a feast of remembrance, when we remember the great miracles that took place when Moses led our people our of slavery in Egypt. The sacrifice of the lambs was for protection and the Lord spared the lives of our firstborn sons in Egypt. But he reminded me of the night when Jesus shared the bread and the wine with His disciples. The cup of wine was a symbol of his blood that would be shed for the forgiveness of our sins. He was our Passover Lamb. So instead of killing a lamb and taking it home to eat with our family, now we gather and share bread and wine. This is instead of that! We observed this feast with them the last time we were here."

"What did he say about Yom Kippur? The bull and the goats are sacrificed for our sins too."

"He did explain that. Jesus came to earth as the Lamb of God and when he died it was the culmination of all the sacrifice for sin throughout history. He was the ultimate sacrifice and we need no more sacrifice for sin."

"Can we continue to go to the temple?"

"The temple is still part of our lives. We go there for teaching and fellowship, to fast and pray and worship our God. But there is no more sacrifice for sin."

Reuben sat for a long time thinking about all these things. *Did that mean they would no longer set apart some of their lambs for the temple?*

"I am ready to go to the temple," he said, standing up and preparing to leave the house. "I understand the difference now. I wish all Israelites realized that the Lamb of God has died once for all."

It was a strange Passover season for Reuben and his new parents. They were thankful to have the fellowship and teaching of their friends who also believed and could answer their questions. The time they spent in their booth, selling robes and blankets, was also spent contemplating what they had learned.

Every chance they got Ethan, Judith and Reuben gathered with those of The Way at Solomon's Porch and one or another of Jesus' disciples passed on to them what Jesus taught while he was on earth. Often it was James who was teaching and telling them about the miracles still being done in Jesus' name and answering any questions they had.

Judith had a question.

"I am a weaver. When Jesus was crucified, the soldiers cast lots for his cloak. I saw that garment, woven without a seam, like a priest's robe. What does that mean? Jesus was from David's line, not the priestly line of Levi."

"Do you remember hearing about the time when our father Abram met Melchizedek?" James asked in answer to her question. "Abram had won a great battle and Melchizedek, the king of Salem and a priest of God went out to meet him and blessed him. Abram gave Melchizedek a tenth of all the goods he had recovered. What did that mean?"

"A tenth is the tithe that is given to the priest. Was Melchizedek a priest?" someone asked.

"Our Torah says he was a priest of God Most High. He was the king of Salem, our Jerusalem. Melchizedek means *King of Justice* and since Salem means peace, he was also *King of Peace.*"

"But who was he? Where did he come from? What tribe?" Ethan asked.

"There is no record of his father or mother, no beginning or end to his life. But our ancestors believe it was Shem, the son of Noah. Shem lived for over 600 years. He was alive long before the priestly line of Levi was set up but he was still alive during Abram's time and was Abram's ancestor. Jesus was of the lineage of David who descended from Abram."

"Does that make him a priest?"

"King David said about the coming Messiah, '*You are a priest forever in the order of Melchizedek.*' Our human priests all die, but because Jesus is alive again, he is a priest forever."

He is a priest but he only taught in the outer courts. Priests are responsible for presenting the blood but he never went into the Priest's Court, he never entered the Holy of Holies with blood.

Then James made a statement that cleared up some of Reuben's doubt.

"Jesus returned to the Father and personally presented the blood at the throne in heaven. He entered the Most Holy place of all."

"Many people are believing the teaching of Jesus," Andrew's father explained later as the two families ate a meal together. "We spend time together, we share what we have with people in need and we worship and pray together."

"Are you having trouble with the temple authorities?" Ethan asked.

"They are becoming upset and worried as more and more people follow Jesus' teaching. But how can they deny all the miracles?"

✡ ✡ ✡

THE TRIP HOME WAS A TIME for them to discuss all the things they had learned. It would be several months before they would be back in the city but they talked about the way they could put into practice the things they had learned.

The flax was waiting for them. Reuben was surprised to learn that inside each stem were about twenty flat, yellowish fibres about two feet long but to access it all that woody shell around them had to scutched or beaten away. Reuben had his first experience with beating the flax straw. Then Judith guided him through the next step, combing the fibres with a hackle to remove the last of the unwanted bits and pieces of the stalk. He was still eager to learn so he worked at the job until all the fibres were free of debris and ready for his mother to prepare for spinning.

"Working with the linen fibres is different than working with wool." Judith demonstrated as she pulled the fibres apart into the thickness she wanted. "I overlap them end to end, splice them with a twist and roll them into a ball, splicing and adding threads as I go along. A ball of linen thread is like a roleg of wool, ready to spin."

Finally she sent Reuben out to help his father with the barley harvest so he would learn that process as well. His father was using the scythe on the portion of the crop that had been designated weeks ago as their first fruit offering. As he harvested that area he had Reuben add it to the fleece and flax already set aside as first fruits.

"Will we take them to the temple at Shavuot?" Reuben asked.

"I hope by then your mother will have her purple wool spun and ready to take also. That's five weeks away. Our harvest should be done and we can take it all."

Reuben slowly learned the rhythm of the scythe until he could take turns with his father in both the cutting and bundling of the hairy bristling sheaves. By the end of the day they had half the field cut.

"What will we do with all these sheaves when we are finished here?" Reuben questioned.

"See that flat area on top of the hill," his father said, pointing to a flat circle, bare and hard packed amidst the poppies and daisies around about them. "That's what we use as a threshing floor. It's high enough to catch the prevailing winds to blow the chaff away, and flat enough to grind the heads under the sled."

The following evening they began threshing. Ethan hitched the donkey to a sled made of two heavy boards. Then he covered the threshing floor with loose sheaves and showed Reuben how to guide the animal back and forth, over the grain. Reuben watched the scene change around him. As the golden sheaves were crushed and ground under the sled, gusts of wind sent chaff billowing through the air, turning everything yellow. Piles of barley kernels soon took the place of the sheaves. Later that would all be winnowed, sifted and stored in pottery jars Ethan explained. Reuben grinned when he saw his father, covered with husks and stubble as the evening breeze blew the dry chaff around and changed his hair from black to gold.

Reuben laughed out loud as he helped to winnow the grain, tossing it into the air so more debris would blow away as the heavier grain kernels fell to the ground. Dry chaff clung to the perspiration on his skin, making him uncomfortable and itchy, like a million little gnats crawling on him. The day's job was finished when the remaining straw was heaped in piles to be used for bedding for the sheep or for making bricks. "I will sleep out here and guard our harvest tonight," Reuben offered. "I'm used to sleeping outside."

It was a quiet, warm night as Reuben settled down, cushioning his arms behind his head for a pillow and watched the stars above. Only once did he hear rustling nearby, but when he shouted the noise faded away. *That might have been someone wanting to steal our grain, but it might have been an animal too. I'm glad I was here.*

He watched the moon follow its course and thought about how much the lives of his people and their worship related to the orbit of the moon. This year had been a regular year, but every two or three years, an extra month would be added to make sure Passover took place in the spring.

✡ ✡ ✡

When the barley harvest was finally over and the grain stored away it was time to harvest the wheat and the same process began again. In all this time Reuben had rarely seen his grandfather. He led the sheep to pasture every morning and only when they were at the threshing floor did Reuben see him in the distance bringing the sheep home.

"This would be a good time for us to gather as Followers of the Way do in Jerusalem," Ethan mentioned to Noam.

"Nina is helping Ayla so I can come to your house." So Noam came to his son's home and the four of them talked about the Messiah.

"The believers worship, eat and pray together," Ethan stated. "Each one shares a song or a Psalm. So maybe that's a good way for us to start."

Noam began to sing and as each one recognized the Psalm he had chosen they joined in, their four voices sending worship in song heavenward.

"*O, Lord, hear me as I pray; pay attention to my groaning. Listen to my cry for help, my King and my God, for I pray to no one but you. Listen to my voice in the morning, Lord. Each morning I bring my requests to you and wait expectantly.*"

They sang through the entire Psalm and certain parts of it planted themselves in Reuben's mind. "*Because of your unfailing love, I can enter your house; I will worship at your Temple with deepest awe. Lead me in the right path, O Lord, or my enemies will conquer me. Make your way plain for me to follow.*"

"It is because of God's unfailing love that I can enter his house," Reuben stated with surprise in his voice. "When I was a leper I could not go into the temple."

"Your healing is something we can praise the Lord for," Ethan suggested. "And your mother's healing. Andrew's father said the believers pray together too."

"The man who shaved me at the Serpent's Pool prayed for me before he left," Reuben said with wonder in his voice. "I had never heard anyone pray like that before. His prayer was one of worship and praise but it came from his heart."

"There are many places in our Torah readings where people prayed like that," Noam replied. "When Abraham prayed for the Lord to rescue Lot and save Sodom and when Hannah prayed for a son. Many of the Psalms are prayers from David's heart."

"I prayed from my heart when I was asking the Lord for a child," Judith confessed. "But maybe we shouldn't wait until we are in despair to pray from the heart."

"That man's prayer was not recited from his memory," Reuben stated. "He asked the Lord to bless me and make me a blessing to many. Maybe once we begin it will get easier." Bowing his head, Reuben prayed a simple prayer of worship and thanksgiving.

"O, Lord, my King and my God," Judith prayed with fervency. "Thank you for giving me a new son. You have already answered that man's prayer because Reuben is a great blessing to us."

Tears were freely flowing down their faces by the time they had finished pouring out their praise and thanksgiving to their creator.

"Now I understand why the believers love to gather together," Ethan whispered.

"We have worshipped and prayed. Now we must eat!" Judith rose and soon had an ample supply of food on the table.

"We will remember the Lord in our eating too, like the apostles told us to do." Ethan led them in remembering the body and blood of their Messiah as they ate bread and shared a cup of wine. They agreed that they would do this again, often.

Chapter 15

"I HAVE LIVED HERE in Bethlehem for a year already." Now that the harvest was complete Reuben once again joined his sabba sat on the side of a hill. "I have learned how to harvest fruit and grain, how to shear a sheep and look after the flock. I have even learned how much work goes into making our clothing."

"You have been a good helper. Your father often speaks of how happy he is to have you for a son, and how much he loves you."

"He does? I love him too, and my mother, and you and Savtah. God has poured blessing upon blessing upon us."

WHISPERED RUMOURS WERE CIRCULATING around Bethlehem. People were secretly going to Jerusalem and finding healing. When and who was never revealed.

"It reminds me of when Jair was born and stories about angels, stars and magi were being told in the village," Judith told Reuben.

Quietly they talked, wondering about the connection between the birthplace of the infant king, the healing ministry of the Messiah, the crucifixion and resurrection of the Lamb of God.

"Is all this part of God's plan?" Reuben questioned.

"We have a lot of questions to ask when we return to Jerusalem for Shavuot"

Reuben was unusually quiet on the trip to the city, thinking about his friends, Andrew and Tirus. It was only fifty days since he had seen them at Passover but still he missed them.

They were busy arranging robes and blankets for display when Andrew and his father showed up at their booth in front of the inn. Reuben was glad to see Andrew. They all sat down together on the steps of the inn and Ethan quietly asked what was going on. Amazing stories began to unfold.

"Peter and John saw a beggar being left to beg for alms by the Beautiful Gate." Reuben remembered the decorated ceiling inside that double gate.

"When he asked for alms, Peter told him he didn't have money but he would give him what he had." In a hushed voice Andrew's father continued. "Peter took the man by the hand and told him to stand up and walk in the name of Jesus Christ the Nazarene."

"What happened?" Reuben asked.

"The man was instantly healed and began praising God."

"We have heard rumours that even people from Bethlehem are coming here for healing," Ethan remarked. "The number of believers must be growing every day."

"We now number over five thousand. But that was a terrifying time. Hundreds of people soon gathered around them and Peter told them they had rejected Jesus, the Messiah, the author of life, and had him put to death. He told them too that God had raised Jesus from the dead and now faith in His name had healed this man."

"Ahhh! The work of the Messiah continues."

"But the Sadducees were furious because they do not believe in the resurrection of the dead. The temple leaders arrested Peter and John and put them in jail overnight. The next day the council met and asked them by what means they had done this miracle and Peter told them the same thing all over again. The man who had been healed was standing right there, so they had no choice but to let Peter and John go but they warned them and threatened them to never again speak or teach in the name of Jesus."

"What did the apostles do? Have they stopped preaching?"

"We all met together and prayed and asked the Lord to hear their threats and give all of us great boldness in preaching and that healings, miracles, signs and wonders would be done in Jesus' name. The result has been a great unity amongst the followers of the Messiah. The very thing Jesus prayed for before his death, that we all would be one as he and the father are one, has happened."

"So all is well?"

"The Lord answered our prayers and there have been so many miracles and healings in Jesus' name."

"Praise be to God."

"Yes, but they arrested the apostles again and put them in jail."

Reuben felt his heart rejoicing and then plunged into despair as the stories unfolded, victories and defeats one after another. What would come next? He didn't have to wait long as Andrew began to add more.

"The most amazing thing happened. An angel came one night and opened the gates of the jail and told the apostles to go back and teach in the temple. The temple leaders were irate but they didn't know what to do. Did you know the Sanhedrin doesn't even meet on the Temple Mount anymore."

"Did they arrest the Apostles again?"

"Do you remember once seeing the great teacher, Gamaliel, with all his students?" Andrew 's father took up the story "He is a very wise man. He told the members of the Sanhedrin that if this movement was of God, they best beware about fighting against God. But he also said if it was just people doing it themselves, it would soon disappear. They listened to him and let the apostles go."

Reuben breathed a huge sigh of relief and heard his parents exhale heavily as well. They had a wonderful time with other believers and by the time they returned home to Bethlehem they were excited and enthusiastic about what was happening in Jerusalem. The dry season was upon them and at once they were busy harvesting figs, dates and olives. This year Reuben could do everything a little faster than the previous year.

"Look at all the fruit," he exclaimed, remembering the hard work they had done in the spring. "Now I understand how important it was to climb the trees and move the male flowers over into the female trees."

The stories he had heard rolled over and over in his mind as he worked. He could hardly wait to return to the city and hear more about the thousands of people who were hearing and believing the truth about the Messiah. This year, because his savtah was not well they didn't go to Jerusalem for Rosh Hashanah, but went a bit later in time only for Yom Kippur and the first few days of the Feast of Tabernacles.

Andrew's family invited them to celebrate the feast with them again and they had a wonderful time together in their roof-top booth. They celebrated Yom Kippur together but when they were preparing to leave the city they received astonishing news that made Reuben's heart leap as it did the day they heard that Jesus had risen from the dead.

"What does this mean? So many strange things have taken place. This must mean something special." Reuben and his father had just finished loading their belongings onto the donkey but now they stood, stunned into silence at the news Tirus had given them.

"Tell us again," Ethan stated.

"The news is spreading all around the city even though the temple leaders are trying to hush it up. The man who took the scapegoat to the edge of the wilderness this year

Chapter 16

REUBEN DECIDED THAT whenever he took a turn sitting beside his *savtah* he would talk to her about the Psalm for that day. Just as they read through the Torah every year at Synagogue, they also read through the Psalms from New Moon to New Moon.

"This Psalm is for you, *Savtah*," Reuben stated one day. "In peace I will lie down and sleep, for you alone, O Lord, will keep me safe."

"Thank you, Reuben," his grandmother whispered. "I will sleep now." Reuben continued to sit by her side as she napped.

What can I do? I want Savtah to believe in the Messiah before she dies. But she won't even let me talk about him. I wonder what has made her so sad all her life. That was when he remembered Noam telling him about all their babies who had died.

Two days later, Reuben began quoting the twenty-second Psalm to her. Age-weary eyes focused on him. Sentence after sentence rolled off his tongue. The Psalmist talked about being scorned and despised, surrounded by his enemies, his tongue sticking to the roof of his mouth.

"*Savtah*, when I watched Jesus of Nazareth being crucified He quoted some of this Psalm." Reuben was quivering in fear that he would offend, but the urge to tell her what he had seen could not be held back. "This Psalm, My God, My God, why have you forsaken me. Then he says they have pierced my hands and feet. I can count all my bones. My life is poured out like water and all my bones are out of joint. My enemies throw dice for my clothing." Reuben grasped her hand as he knelt beside her cot.

"*Savtah*, Jesus' hands and feet were pierced when he was nailed to the cross. He was also thirsty and asked for a drink but most unusual is that the Roman guards cast lots for his cloak. Judith told me she saw that garment and it was woven without a seam, like a priest's robe."

Reuben looked at his grandmother and her eyes were closed but softly he added one more statement. "Before he died, Jesus cried out, 'My God, my God, why have you forsaken me?'"

On the Sabbath Noam sat with her while the other three went to synagogue and then Reuben volunteered to sit with her the remainder of the day. He was sorry that her illness had drained the expression from her face. She could no longer smile or eat very well. He didn't know if she could even hear him any more, so he sat and talked about things he had seen. He told her the entire story of waking up with leprosy, being sent away when he was not even twelve years old.

He had never told anyone the things he told his *savtah* that day. How it felt to see his fingers and toes disappearing. What it was like to smell so bad that no one wanted to be near him.

But then he told her how Ethan, Judith and Tirus had been kind to him. Jumping to his feet he walked around the small room as he told her about the day when Jesus touched him and healed him. Joy rang out in his voice as he described how he counted ten fingers and ten toes.

"Did I tell you, *Savtah*, that I walked all the way to Galilee just to see Jesus after he came alive again? With my own eyes I saw him die and the Roman guards even pierced his side with a sword to prove he was dead but with my own eyes I saw him alive again in Galilee. After all those things I knew he was my Messiah." Then he told her the story he had told Noam, about the scapegoat and what it meant.

Reuben left when Ethan came to take his place and sit beside his mother. When Ethan came home only a couple hours later Reuben knew the worst had happened but the expression on Ethan's face was a surprise.

"My mother woke for a few minutes and was trying to say something but her voice was so very weak. I finally understood her. She wanted me to give you a message, Reuben."

"Really? A message for me? What did she say?"

"She said to tell you that *The Lamb of God takes away sin.*"

✡ ✡ ✡

Ethan prayed Kaddish for his mother for the first time that day and Reuben knew he would repeat it every month for eleven months. It was a beautiful prayer that had no mention of death in it, but only praise to the Lord for all his blessings. Reuben knew that when the time came, he would pray Kaddish for his mother and father too.

"I once heard someone remark that each member of our family is a gift from the Lord, a blessing for us to hold for him for a time" Judith told them. "When it is time for that one to return to the Lord, it is good for us to give him praise. Job said, 'The Lord giveth and the Lord taketh away, blessed be the name of the Lord.'"

Reuben was surprised at the next thought that invaded his mind.

"No one has to pray Kaddish for the Messiah, because he came back to life again." Noam placed his hand on Reuben's head as he so often did when a profound statement came out of his young mouth.

✡ ✡ ✡

"It is time for you to move into my house," Noam stated one day as he ate the evening meal with the family."

"Why should we do that?" Ethan asked in amazement.

"My house is bigger. It has the room you built. It is also closer to the sheep and the fields and I am not able to help as much as before."

The family talked about that idea for several days, until Ethan realized his father wanted to move away from the memories. The following day they worked all day moving their possessions. The hardest thing to move was the loom.

"This is the room I built," Ethan told Reuben as they worked to put the loom back together. "This will be our room and you can have the room where my parents slept. Now your mother won't wake you in the morning when she starts making barley loaves."

Reuben was now eighteen years old and had grown strong over the years so this year he had no difficulty ploughing, planting and harvesting. It had been two years since he came to live with Ethan and Judith in Bethlehem. It was his home.

The next time Reuben returned to the city he went alone. He hurried to the temple to meet his friends of The Way but as he approached he saw the worry in their faces.

"What is happening?" He whispered to a man he knew who was a believer.

"Stephen has been teaching and performing wonderful miracles. Now, out of fear, or jealousy, or anger, men have made him a target of their vendetta. Men, from the Synagogue of the Freed Slaves, have brought false accusations against Stephen and he has been arrested and taken before the Sanhedrin"

Reuben was aware that there were dozens of synagogues in Jerusalem. It was convenient for Israelites living in various regions outside of Israel to have their own synagogue in Jerusalem where they could meet together when they came to the city for the feast days. How could anyone tell lies like that?

Reuben moved along with Stephen's friends to where they could hear what was happening. He was thankful that several situations had caused the Sanhedrin to meet outside the temple where they could now watch. Stephen stood in front of the council.

Stephen is highly educated, unlike many of the apostles who were uneducated. He is also an eloquent speaker. He will make them understand.

Stephen identified with the men of the council, addressing them as brethren and fathers. Reuben saw Gamaliel sitting with the council and remembered how wise the man was when he advised the Sanhedrin before. With him was one of his students, a man named Saul.

Reuben listened closely as Stephen reviewed the entire history of their nation, beginning with their humble beginnings when God called Abraham. He reminded them of Isaac who eventually had to go to Egypt to save his family and then four hundred years later the Lord raised up Moses.

Reuben stiffened. This was the charge against Stephen, of speaking against the teachings of Moses.

"Our own people rejected Moses saying, 'Who has made you a ruler and judge over us?' Yet Moses led them out of Egypt with many signs and wonders and miracles. Moses himself told the people of Israel, 'God will raise up for you a Prophet like me from among your own people.'"

Reuben listened eagerly as Stephen told of the Tabernacle, constructed according to God's plan, that they carried with them for generations, until the time of King

David when he wanted to build a house for God. Reuben was confused when Stephen told them that God does not dwell in a building made by man.

What does he mean? What is he saying about The Temple? Then Stephen quoted from Isaiah, "Heaven is my throne, and the earth is my footstool. Could you build me a temple as good as that? asks the Lord." Reuben's heart dropped within him.

Was Stephen speaking against the temple?

He didn't have time to dwell on that thought because Stephen's next statement was scathing.

"Name one prophet your ancestors didn't persecute! They even killed the ones who predicted the coming of the Righteous One, the Messiah who you betrayed and killed."

That was as much as the religious leaders could take. In anger and fury they shook their fists at him but Stephen looked up and said, "Look, I see the heavens opened and the Son of Man standing in the place of honor at God's right hand!"

Reuben gasped. *James spoke the truth. Jesus did present his blood at the throne.*

What followed was unimaginable to Reuben. Stephen was grabbed, hauled outside of the city and stoned. But as Stephen fell to his knees he shouted, "Lord, don't charge them with this sin." And then he died. It reminded Reuben of Jesus on the cross crying out, "Father, forgive them, for they know not what they do."

Within days Reuben had returned to Bethlehem, in sorrow, and yes, even in fear.

"Things are not going well in Jerusalem," he told his parents. "The believers are under much persecution and Stephen has been stoned to death. Saul is going everywhere dragging out believers and they are scattering in every direction. Then he told them what Stephen had told the leaders.

"I understand so much more now. Remember the story Jesus told about the man leaving his vineyard in the hands of renters who killed all the servants who came to collect his due for him and finally killed the owner's son as well. It was the history of what our ancestors have done, killing all the prophets and finally even the Son of God."

"We will not go back to Jerusalem for a while," Ethan stated. "We must stay here where it is safe."

A LOUD POUNDING on the door wakened Reuben.

"Ethan, wake up!"

Reuben recognized the hoarse whisper of Jacob and, rolling off his mat, he quickly opened the door to let the man in.

"Where is Ethan? You have to leave right away. You and Ethan."

"Jacob? What's the matter?" Ethan came from the other room with his hair tousled, rubbing sleep from his eyes.

"You and Reuben have to leave immediately. That Pharisee, Saul, has been arresting and killing Christians in Jerusalem and a lot of other places. Now he's on his way to

Bethlehem. He's almost at the edge of the village. People in Bethlehem know you and Reuben are followers of Jesus the Messiah, even though you have been quiet about it. They have seen it in your life. Run to the hills as fast as you can. Don't take time to gather anything, just run."

"What about Judith?"

"Hannah will hide her at our house. They won't be looking there for followers of The Way, but we don't have room for all three of you. Hurry! He has a lot of men with him who will spread out as soon as they get into Bethlehem."

Judith appeared as Reuben and Ethan were putting on their outer garments. Having heard everything Jacob said, Judith handed Reuben a robe she had taken off the loom the evening before. Then she piled blankets and another robe into Ethan's arms.

"It is just like the night Herod came to kill Jair," Judith whispered. Ethan put an arm around her shaking shoulders as she reached for Reuben and pulled him into her embrace. "Go with God, Kaddish. Don't be afraid. That was a horrible time but God used it to protect our Messiah. Somehow He will protect you too. Run! Both of you. Here, take this with you." She placed a linen bag in Reuben's hand and pushed him towards the door.

Reuben slipped out the door with Ethan close behind. They glanced back to see Jacob escort Judith in the other direction.

Chapter 17

REUBEN ALLOWED ETHAN to move ahead of him in the darkness and followed him down the hill, past the sheepfold and along the path they used everyday to take the sheep to pasture. Before they were to the top of the hill they heard the shouts of Saul's men banging on doors. Ethan pulled Reuben down into a crouch so their silhouettes wouldn't be seen above the hill. Veering they ran, hunched over, just below the crest of the hill.

When they finally paused to catch their breath Ethan put his arm around Reuben.

"I know every cave and cleft in these rocks," he stated. "There is a cave up ahead that goes deep into the hill. We will hide there for tonight."

Reuben could hardly see his father but clutched the edge of his robe as he moved stealthily ahead of him. *If I can't see him then the ones who are looking for us won't be able to see us either.*

Reuben felt his father take hold of his arm as the ground under his feet changed. He knew at once that they were in a cave, a huge cave by the slight echo of the patter of their feet on limestone.

"I can't see anything," Reuben whispered.

"Neither can I. We'll just go a bit farther before we settle down for the night. The cave turns a corner just ahead of us."

Reuben had his hand on the wall of the cave and knew when they turned left and were out of sight of the entrance of the cave.

"This is good."

Reuben sensed his father had lowered himself to the ground so he settled down with his back against the cave wall.

"Put on that extra robe and here's a blanket to wrap around you on top of that. Cover your head too. It's cool in here. We should try and sleep. Tomorrow we'll decide what to do."

The next morning they recited broche together and then looked into the bag Judith had given Ethan as they left the house. It was a treasure chest of necessities: barley loaves, figs, grapes and olives. Wrapped in a linen cloth were strips of dried fish and mutton.

Their stomachs were soon filled and they turned their attention to what lay ahead. In low voices they talked about what they should do in various situations.

"If one of us is caught, the other one should hide, no matter which one of us it is," Ethan stated. "One of us must be strong for Mama."

"I know how to be still so no one sees me," Reuben replied. "I had lots of practice doing that. But I also know a way to keep people away. Some time I will show you."

The sun gradually warmed the outside air and the cave began to warm up. Suddenly they heard a rustling out on the hill and the sound grew louder until it sounded like many feet. Reuben gripped his father's arm as he heard someone approach the mouth of the cave. Then silence settled once again upon the hillside.

Reuben peeked around the stone wall that separated them from the entrance.

"It's *Sabba*! He has a lamb in his lap and the sheep are on the hillside." Reuben moved to run towards his beloved Noam.

"No!" His father whispered. "Someone may have followed him."

"Now, little lamb, you stay close to me so you don't wander off and get hurt," Noam stated. "I know you are both in the cave. Are you okay?"

"We're fine, *Sabba*," Reuben replied softly. "Mama sent food with us and blankets."

"Good. I have more food and water that I will leave here when I return home, but don't come out for it until dark. Saul and his men are still in Bethlehem, going from door to door. Six people have already been arrested and taken to Jerusalem."

"Six? There were six other believers in the village?" Ethan questioned.

"More than that, but many are hiding in the hills, just like you. If I find them I will send them here. This is the biggest cave in the area."

Noam sat outside the cave, never letting on that he was talking to anyone other than the lamb. He told them Judith was safe.

"How do you know about this cave?" Reuben finally asked, curiosity getting the better of him.

"The Maccabees were in power a long time ago, even before I was born and they set up what we called the Hasmonean kingdom," Noam replied softly, directing his voice towards the lamb. "My family lived in Jerusalem in that time." Noam stood up and walked away to guide a ewe back to the flock. Then he sat down again.

"Two Jewish brothers, Hyrcanus II and Aristobulus II fought over which of them would hold the position of high priest. It got so bad that finally both of them appealed to Rome to intervene and settle their power struggle. I'm sure those two brothers had no idea what their family squabble would mean to our people."

"Rome sent Pompey the Great, a Roman general, to Jerusalem to settle the matter. He killed our priests right at the altar and then he and his men began to slaughter people in Jerusalem. My family fled the city and eventually hid in this cave. Pompey and his army killed 12,000 Jews and Rome has ruled over our nation ever since."

"How did you know about the cave if you weren't born yet?" Reuben questioned again.

"My family never went back to live in Jerusalem. We settled here in Bethlehem and my father told me the story and showed me this cave and I, in turn, showed it to my son," Noam replied. "This cave saved our family once: it will do so again."

The trio continued to chat softly as Noam sat outside the cave pretending to talk to the lamb he cuddled and petted. For a while he practiced with his sling. Reuben wished he could be out there with him. *Sabba taught me how to use the sling and we had so much fun together.* Several times Noam walked away to herd a stray sheep back to the flock. Finally it was time for him to take the flock home.

"God be with you," he said as he left. "I will return tomorrow."

Every day he came to sit in front of the cave while the flock grazed nearby. Every time he left, there was a linen bag of food tucked under a nearby shrub. They retrieved the food after dark and one or the other picked their way in the dark to a nearby stream for water.

One night a rustling in the dark woke them.

"Listen to me. Don't be afraid," a voice whispered from the entrance of the cave. "Are you there, Ethan?"

"I am here," Ethan whispered back.

"Noam sat outside the small cave where we were hiding and told us there would be room for us here with you."

Reuben could tell by the sounds that several people entered the cave and felt their way along the wall until they turned the corner.

"Just sit down where you are," Ethan replied, "and in the morning we will find more space for you. There's lots of room."

Reuben was surprised when he woke up in the morning and saw seven people curled up in their blankets. Only one was awake. Sparkling brown eyes stared at him from under a robe. Reuben smiled and a timid smile was returned. The robe slipped down and Reuben gasped when he saw the soft curls and gentle features of a girl. Yakira!

It was a joyful but quiet reunion between the two families when everyone was awake and they were introduced to another couple who had come with them. Reuben was glad to have Andrew there and to hear about their search for safety as Saul attempted to rid Jerusalem of followers of the Messiah.

The atmosphere inside the cave took on a new feeling. Yakira and Sheera helped the women prepare their meagre rations. Reuben and Andrew talked for hours on end, Andrew telling Reuben how Jerusalem had become a place of terror and the temple porches were avoided. Now and then Reuben and Yakira talked, sharing their fears of the future.

"What are you doing up there, old man?" A shout came from below one day as Noam sat by the door of the cave while just out of sight people scurried to pick up everything they could find and rush further back into the cave.

"Watching my sheep. I bring them up here every day."

"What's in that cave?"

Footsteps came inside the cave and around the corner where they had been sitting moments ago. A torch lit up the inside of the cave and the single person who appeared in the flickering light.

Chapter 18

THE PEOPLE HAD BARELY had time to move farther back in the cave and out of sight. Only Reuben remained and he was ready for them.

"Unclean! Unclean!" He called out in a hoarse voice.

"It's a leper!" The men screamed as the light of the torch illuminated the figure crouched in front of them. In a panic they turned and rushed out of the cave. "There's a leper in there," they yelled at Noam and went running down the hillside, scraping their sandals on tufts of grass to wipe off any cave dust that might contaminate them.

Reuben walked towards the mouth of the cave, grinning as he watched them race down the hill. As the others came from the back of the cave everyone chuckled when they saw him. With his blanket pulled up over his head, he had thrown dust and clumps of dirt over himself. His face and hands were streaked with grime but his white teeth gleamed from his smiling mouth.

"You are a very wise son," Ethan stated and patted Reuben on the back.

"That was what I meant when I said I knew how to keep people away. I never thought that leprosy could ever be a blessing."

They joined together in praising God for saving them, Noam still outside the cave and the others just inside.

"I don't think I can come back here again," Noam said sadly. "Now that they think there's a leper in the cave they would wonder why I would risk my life to come back but you should be safe here now. Those men won't be back and somehow we will find a way to bring food."

Noam called to his sheep and started down the hillside, the sheep following obediently behind him. The lamb that had been in his lap day after day now frisked along beside him, leaping and skipping down the hill.

Occasionally Noam brought them news and there was always food under the shrub although Reuben and Ethan never saw him bring it. He also continued to direct other families to their shelter. They would arrive in the dark of night, calling out in whispers from the mouth of the cave.

Then one day Noam came and sat outside their cave again and informed them that Saul had gone back to Jerusalem, but some of his men remained in the village still searching for Christians.

By the time he brought word that all of Saul's men had left Jerusalem and the surrounding area, there were forty-seven people living in the cave. Though they were relieved at the news and their first instinct was to rush out, they first worshipped together, praising God for protecting them through this time of trial, before they left the cave and moved into the brightness outside.

Slowly, thin and emaciated, they all began to return to their homes but it was a long time before they felt safe again. Judith cried when Ethan and Reuben returned home and they were together again. Jacob and Hannah had hidden her well.

Reuben's eyes were overflowing as he said good-bye to Andrew as their family left but his greatest heartache was watching Yakira leave. He treasured the few times they had been alone and talked about the future. *I wonder when I will see her again.* Then he remembered the Psalm their family had sung at their very first gathering as believers, and it became his prayer. *Lead me in the right path, O Lord, or my enemies will conquer me. Make your way plain for me to follow.*

THINGS WOULD NEVER BE THE SAME in Bethlehem again. Reuben saw empty homes from which families had fled to other places of refuge, leaving everything behind, never to return. A cloud of fear hovered over the village, no one knowing if Saul and his men would return.

"SOMEONE HAS BEEN ASKING FOR YOU." Jacob whispered to Reuben a few days later as he passed him in the village street. "He said he is your sister's husband. I told him I would ask people to see if you still lived here and he should come back later to see me."

"I do have a sister and the last time I saw her she was planning to marry. Tell him my sister must come to see you. I will be hidden nearby and if it is Deborah, my sister, I will come and talk to her."

As he hurried home Reuben was filled with conflicting emotions. *Saul's people have gone but have they sent a spy to find me and tell Saul's people so they could arrest me? Has someone come to inform me that my father or mother has died?*

Judith tried to calm him. "Maybe it is your sister. It has been a long time since you left home, no longer suffering with leprosy. Perhaps she has come looking for you to make sure you are still well. Jacob will let us know when she comes."

A few hours later Jacob sent word that the woman would be at his door before sundown.

"Do you want me to go with you?" Ethan asked.

"No! I don't want you nearby in case there is danger. Jacob will come and tell you if anything happens to me."

"God watch over you."

Reuben sat down on the ground near Jacob's house, in the familiar beggar's position, arms folded on bent knees, head down on his arms. With his head covered but his face turned towards Jacob's house he could see anyone who came near.

Reuben had a difficult time staying on the ground when a woman came slowly down the lane. Without question it was his sister, Deborah, older, yes, and with sadness and fear in her eyes. Jacob came outside to talk to her so Reuben could hear their conversation.

"Have you found my brother, Reuben?" Deborah asked. "He is still here in Bethlehem, yes?"

"Why did you say you were looking for him? Do you have news for him?"

"Yes, I have news that will make him happy and make him sad."

"Have you come to harm him?"

"No! I have come in love. We have come to live in Bethlehem if he is still here."

Reuben couldn't control his excitement any more. He leaped up and hurried towards his sister.

"Deborah! Is it really you?" The pair embraced and Reuben was surprised to see tears in her eyes as he stepped back. She glanced in fear at Jacob.

"This is my friend, Jacob. He was trying to protect me."

"He is a good protector. He made me think you had moved away from here."

"Tell me all." Reuben urged and was surprised when his sister hugged him again and began to sob.

"Are you still a follower of The Way?" She whispered in his ear when she finally got control of her emotions.

"Why do you ask?"

"We have been living in Jerusalem and my husband, Obed, and I have come to believe that Jesus of Nazareth is

Messiah." His sister still spoke into Reuben's ear in a whisper.

"Yes, we follow The Way." Reuben wasn't afraid to speak the words out loud. He hugged his sister again and now tears of happiness were in his own eyes. "We spent many weeks hiding in a cave while that man, Saul, had his men here hunting for believers." Reuben put his hand on Jacob's shoulder. "Jacob, our friend helped us. You have a family?"

"Yes. We fled from Saul's hatred too and we have been hiding outside of Bethlehem all this time until we knew it was safe for us to come. Our son is weak and sick. There were people hiding with us who remembered you from Jerusalem. They saw your friend Andrew along the road and he told us where you were."

"You saw Andrew?"

"Yes. He and his family are going to live with his father's family in Perga."

"We must go right away and bring your family into the village. They will be worried about you. My mother will nurse them back to health."

Reuben saw the surprised look that crossed Deborah's face when he called Judith his mother.

"Yes, Deborah, I was adopted by a wonderful couple here who needed a son just when I needed a family. You will meet them. We will worship with them. Do we need to take the donkey?" His sister shook her head.

"I will send Hannah to your house," Jacob stated, "so Judith will be ready for you when you get home."

Reuben followed his sister out of the village and up into the hills where her husband, Obed, rushed to meet them. Reuben liked the man as soon as he saw him, delighted at the love and concern he showed for his small family. But Reuben worried as he heard their baby struggling for breath. Reuben helped Obed with the few bags they had been able to gather as they fled from their home, and Deborah carried little Jesse, patting his back, helping him breathe.

"You are coming to our house where you will be safe," Reuben explained to Obed. "We have many years to talk about. Is our mother well? Our father? How are Judah and Perez?" He was still asking questions as they entered the house.

Water was boiling on the hearth and Judith had a wool blanket already warmed to wrap around the baby. Reuben noticed that Deborah hung back shyly as Judith came forward to meet his sister but she was soon as captivated by Judith's kindness as he himself had been. When she handed Deborah a mixture of warm honey and lemon to ease the baby's cough, Reuben knew his mother had won his sister's heart. The baby's cough soothed in response to the warm, sweet liquid that trickled down his throat and before long he slept.

As they gathered later to eat, Ethan recognized the importance of this meal and nodded to Reuben with a smile. Reuben, in a rich, melodic voice offered *motzi.* He could tell that Deborah and Obed were grateful for food. *I just blessed the food in my own home, with my own sister and her family at the table. I give you praise, Jehovah. You are so good.*

Reuben moved his pallet out to the living area so Deborah's family could sleep in the privacy of his room. Even before they all retired for the night Judith and Ethan had made it apparent that they considered this young couple a part of the family. *We must find a house for them. I wonder what Obed does to make a living?* It took a long time for Reuben to drift off to sleep as he thought about having his sister living nearby.

Ethan visited Jacob early the next day to let him know everything was well. Jacob was aware of everything that happened in Bethlehem and by the end of the day he had found a vacant house, abandoned by a family fleeing for their lives as Saul's men invaded their village. He arranged with the village leaders for Obed and his family to live there.

"I'm sure someone has also moved into our vacated house in Jerusalem," Deborah remarked, "and now the Lord has provided us with a home someone else left behind." Noam was generous in giving them pots and utensils that he no longer used since Ayla's death.

As the weeks passed Reuben was happy to see his sister settled in her own home and the baby thriving. Obed was a sandal maker, having learned from Reuben and Deborah's father. He soon had a steady sandal business in the courtyard of their new home but he also enjoyed learning about the sheep and climbing the trees to harvest figs and dates. Like Reuben, this life was new for him but he loved every minute of it. It was a joy for all of them to gather for worship in their home and also go to synagogue together.

✡ ✡ ✡

REUBEN STRETCHED HIS LEGS out in the sunshine as he sat on a hillside with Obed. They watched Noam carry Jesse around, the toddler waving his hands in excitement whenever they neared one of the sheep. Noam stooped so the toddler could dig his hands into the wool of a lamb, and the old man laughed as the child giggled in glee.

"I love the sheep and obviously my son does too," Obed stated. In the months since they had arrived in Bethlehem, Obed and Deborah had immersed themselves in every aspect of Reuben's life.

"I remember the first time I watched Noam with the sheep." Reuben said with a far away look in his eyes as he remembered that day. "I was surprised to find out that every one of the sheep had a name and Noam knew them all. The first time he allowed me to help with the shearing I was terrified. Now I know all their names too."

"The Lord has blessed you with a wonderful family and we are so grateful that you have included us."

"I'm glad you wanted to stay. Now I have to ask you something but I have not spoken to anyone else about it," Reuben said softly. "You are happy here in Bethlehem? You want to stay, yes?"

"If the Lord so ordains, of course. Bethlehem would be a good place for children to grow up."

"I want to go away for a while."

"You are not happy here anymore?" Obed asked, his eyes widening in shock.

"I want to go and find a wife and bring her back to live in Bethlehem but it would ease my mind if you and Deborah were here to help with the work while I am gone."

"Where will you go? Have you already picked out a wife?"

"Yes. My father has already spoken to her father, so they are waiting for me to come and get her. But she lives far away."

"I am happy for you. Go and be at peace. We will do your share of the work."

That evening when they finished their evening meal, Reuben asked his parents to sit with him.

"I have seen how much Noam loves little Jesse. My *sabba* is getting old. He must have lived past eighty years already, yes?" Reuben asked with a smile.

"He is that old and it is hard for him to move around but he does love that little boy," Ethan replied.

"I have been counting up the years of your lives too," Reuben said, looking from Ethan to Judith. "If Jair had lived you would have grandchildren on your knee already."

Reuben saw the glance that passed between them and knew they had also thought about that in the passing years.

"I am young, only nineteen years now, but I want you to have grandchildren to play with and to love before you depart this life. So I would like to leave home for a while to go and get a wife."

"Where will you go?" Judith asked her voice full of concern.

"I will go to Perga and bring Yakira home with me. When we were hiding in the cave, our fathers talked and agreed on a bride price."

Judith looked in shock at her husband, astonished that he knew of this but had not told her.

"It will take me many weeks to go that far and visit them for a few weeks before we come back here again but Obed and Deborah have agreed to help you while I am gone. Will you bless me?"

Quickly his father and mother moved to his side and placed their hands on Reuben's head. Ethan prayed blessings on his trip, his waiting bride and the journey going and coming back.

Two days later Reuben shouldered his provisions for the trip and said good-bye to his parents, *Sabba*, Obed, Deborah and little Jesse.

"I will make one stop on the way," he stated. Looking into Deborah's eyes he continued. "I will stop and see our parents and tell them once more about the Messiah. Pray that their eyes will be open and their hearts will be soft."